Smiling Through
The Apocalypse

To 'The Pages
With all best Wishes
Bonnie J McCafferty
5/93

Bonnie McCafferty

Smiling Through
The Apocalypse

Loose Canons Publishing

Published by

Individual columns in this book first appeared in the author's "Offbeat" column in LOUISVILLE MAGAZINE and are used with permission of LOUISVILLE MAGAZINE.

Other individual columns first appeared in the WOMANEWS section of the CHICAGO TRIBUNE.

Loose Canons Publishing
A division of Creative Resources Inc.
550 West Kentucky Street
Louisville, KY 40203

Cover design by Dan Stewart, Marta Garcia
Cover photo by John Lair

Loose Canons books may be purchased at a special discount for educational, business, or sales promotional use. For information, please call or write: Marketing Department, Loose Canons Publishing, 550 West Kentucky Street, Louisville, KY 40203. Telephone: (502) 584-1810; Fax (502) 585-2814.

First Edition Published 1992

ISBN 0-9634142-0-8

Printed in the United States of America

ACKNOWLEDGMENTS

With all my love to my Mom and Dad, Dee and Cova Lyle; thank you for all the ways you've loved me, and all that you've done for me. Most of all, thank you for always encouraging me to follow my dreams.

To my sister, Carol, who now knows every word in this book by heart, I couldn't have done it without you. Thank you for your love and support and tireless efforts. I love you with all my heart.

With love to Lynn Cralle, Walter Harding and Marty Pollio, who have lived through these pages, and much more, with me. You unfailingly give all the love, support and encouragement that comes with time-honored and time-tested friendship, and for that I am fortunate, and thankful.

My special thanks to Dan Stewart, of Stewart Lopez Bonilla, a good friend and a great designer, who wanted this book to be the best it could be and then made it look better.

Thanks to June Russell for her extra effort and loving care in the typesetting cubicle, thanks to Marta Garcia, who does great cannonball layouts, and thanks to Jason Shepherd who reads well, and carefully.

To my editors, Margaret Carroll at the CHICAGO TRIBUNE and Jack Welch at LOUISVILLE Magazine, thank you for all your help and support; you prove that a good editor is a writer's best friend. And to my first editor at LOUISVILLE Magazine, Bruce Allar, a special thanks for your encouragement and your help.

With love to Bob and Louise Schulman. You're always there for me, and you've always made me be the best I can be. Even when I didn't want to.

Thank you, Bob Hill. You're a good friend, you're an inspiration, and you're very tall.

With love to Alice and Albert Stamper who have everything in-laws should have: dignity, integrity, a sense of humor and a wonderful son.

To my husband, Michael Stamper—thank you for all your untiring efforts to make this book a reality; thank you for making the circle larger, and thank you for proving that, if we can love well only once, then we live well forever.

To
Michael Stamper and Nick Stump
with all my love

CONTENTS

THE MEANING OF LIFE

WOMAN WITH NO BROOM

SMILING THROUGH THE APOCALYPSE

ELVIS IS DEAD AND I KNOW WHY

"It will either work out or it won't."
— Mom

The Meaning Of Life

If Wishes Were Horses

When I was a kid, I wanted a pony. I thought it was important to have a pony since I intended to be a cowboy when I grew up. I also intended to be a writer. I was going to be a writing cowboy—a perfectly consistent career goal in the mind of a five-year-old.

Anyway, my dad was not too keen on the pony idea, so I acquired my riding skills on the neighbor's milk cow. My career as a rodeo rider came to a halt precisely at the same moment our neighbor announced that his milk cow was not producing milk. Without my noble steed, my enthusiasm for cowboyhood diminished.

But I kept on writing, and I kept on dreaming cowboy dreams of freedom. My dreams were so real and so filled with urgent messages to go somewhere that I became a habitual sleepwalker. I spent my nights exploring worlds unknown to me by day, content to be in a state of dream consciousness that was filled with strange but friendly images.

My mom and dad and my sister Carol didn't have a good night's sleep until I went away to college. They all slept half awake, knowing that one of them would have to get up and talk me into going back to bed. Sleepwalkers are like indignant drunks, insisting that they are perfectly fine; in my case, I insisted that I was wide awake— including the night my dad caught me by the ankle and pulled me in off the porch roof.

I'm still not a good sleeper, but dreams still feed my soul whether I'm awake or asleep. When sleep seems impossible, I try to trick myself into drowsiness by playing the wishes game. If I only had one wish, what would I wish for? A thousand more wishes, of course. Okay, smarty, you have a thousand wishes, what do you wish for?

First I get the big stuff out of the way—no more wars, famine, murders, hijackings, plane crashes and no more Republican administrations. And no more homelessness, no child abuse, no AIDS, no cancer—no dread diseases of any kind—and no cavities. And I wish the good teachers and health-care givers would get paid like corporate executives. I wish I were on the bestseller list, and I wish my dog wouldn't drink out of the toilet.

I wish my family and friends and all the people I love, including my dog and my cat, would live forever. Or at least outlive me. And I wish Divine hadn't died. I wish there were more outrageous behavior; I wish we weren't so safe and cautious about life, because there is so little of it. I wish Miscellaneous, my cat, would remember that her litter box is in the basement, and I wish she wouldn't help me type.

I wish all the fanatics in the world had to live together in the same compound and be subjected to 24-hour harangues from television evangelists and Oprah Winfrey. I wish airplanes and restaurants had to give smokers preferred treatment over alcohol-abusers, drug-abusers, racists, anti-Semites, whiners and people who say, "I just work here."

I wish I understood Don King's hair. I wish I could slap Barbara Walters just once for her fawning star-worship. I wish I could have been a close personal friend of Frank Lloyd Wright and Buckminster Fuller and Joan of Arc and Billy the Kid. I wish Minnesota Fats would come by and shoot pool with me. I wish Clint Eastwood would ask me to write a script for him, and I wish *MS.* magazine had a sense of humor. I wish I could talk to Dorothy Parker and Gertrude Stein. I wish I could correspond with Barbara Jordan and Pat Conroy.

I wish I could come to terms completely with my Southern heritage, and I wish the tree in my backyard didn't drop those squashy ugly berries all over my neighbor's new deck. I wish I could listen to 'Amazing Grace' without crying for my granddad, and I wish God would reserve the greatest punishment for those who've ever hurt a child or an old person or an animal.

I wish you could have listened to the message I left on my answering machine for a couple of days not too long ago. It was a short version of Ike and Tina Turner doing 'Proud Mary': "Left a good job in the city, working for the man every night and day; didn't lose a minute of sleep worrying about the way things might have been."

I worked for the man a long time, and for the most part, it was a rewarding experience. I worked hard for my success as a Brown & Williamson marketing executive, and I found out that creativity is rewarded more often than it is punished. I also found out that dreams exist in the corporate world, too. Many of my own dreams came true and many of them didn't. But no matter what happened, I always dreamed of the day I would get up and be completely free to create my own reality.

That day came when I said goodbye to the corporate corridors. It was a beautiful spring day, bright and sunny, full of dogwood blossoms and hope and promise.

A day for wishes and dreams to come true.

The Truth
Shall Set You Free

While I was counting the ways I could maim the person who gave me that ridiculous and lethal salad machine gun for Christmas—the one that sprayed avocado and marinated artichokes all over my dinner guests—it occurred to me that I now possess a profound truth that should be shared before the new year gets too far underway.

Sometime during the course of the last presidential campaign, I began to realize that truths of all kinds seemed to be going out of style, like pine nuts and Jack Russell terriers. So I took up a quest for truth on my own, searching for higher cosmic consciousness and the true meaning of the universe through new-age harmonies and a few games of eightball.

I searched for truth as I cruised around town listening to the lunatic fringe on talk radio shows, and I occasionally sought celestial tutelage from my friend DooDah, psychic guru and paperhanger. DooDah suggested that I would find the key to the universe if I shed my radiant inner light on the darkest path I could find to the bookstore to pick up a few copies of his new book, *How to Have a*

Happy Colon Through Channeling With Crystals.
I was having a little trouble understanding how colons could be made happy with crystals and colored rocks. "Perhaps your colon is already ecstatic," DooDah said without a trace of sarcasm. "Perhaps you should concentrate instead on cleansing the third eye, the one in the mind, of all negative thoughts. Then the truth will appear to you in perfect harmonic convergence and the white bubble on your inner consciousness will…"

"Wait," I said. "Do you mean negative thoughts like if I died and went to hell, I know USAir will fly me there? And the thoughts I have about the woman on my street who leaves parking tickets on my friends' cars? And about self-righteous non-smokers who look for any excuse to be rude?"

"Ah, well," DooDah sighed, gently polishing his glass eye. "You know what your problem is? You simply do not make a distinction between negative thoughts and the desire to kill."

DooDah was about to demonstrate how he had found inner peace through a better $100-bill printing process when he was abruptly hustled away in a familiar car festooned with LPD crests and lots of bells and whistles. Shortly thereafter he sent word through his attorney that he wouldn't be available to counsel me further for one to five, so I was on my own.

Once the presidential election was over, I thought truth was lost forever. So did my accountant when we did my year-end tax review. I was prepared to spend New Year's Eve resolving to seek truth in the halls of academia and at the feet of the unincarcerated, but as it sometimes happens, truth reveals itself in unexpected ways.

I watched the sun rise on Christmas Day in 1988 with my family in the emergency room at Suburban Hospital, thankful for the only Christmas present that mattered: The EMS and cardiology teams there had saved my father's life.

By 8 a.m. his heart beat steadily with the help of a pacemaker, and the flow of blood and oxygen made him bloom again like a spring flower. The twinkle returned to his eyes, and when I bent down to kiss him, he said, "Tell DooDah that life is a gift. At best, life is too short, and the worst offense is to waste it or take it for granted."

DooDah is now happily engaged in learning how to hand-tool wallets, and he recently sent me a message. "Your father speaks the truth," he said. "Life is a gift, and every day we have with the ones we love is a blessing. Wasting life or taking it for granted is an offense worse than passing bogus bills. Happy New Year, and be sure to let me know if you need any money."

Back To The Future

I've been thinking a lot about this decade, and wondering if I'm prepared. The threat of Communism is no longer there to keep me awake questioning whether my crack team of watch animals can stave off a nocturnal nuclear attack (the truth is, a psychopathic cat and an eccentric dog with a bad attitude spend little time thinking about anything other than protecting their respective supper dishes).

Anyway, it is obvious that in the 90's we will mobilize around causes other than the threat of nuclear holocaust: animal rights, vegetable rights, civil rights, the rights of the child, the environment and how to keep James Brown out of jail.

I can only test my preparedness for the 90's by thinking about what I learned in the 80's. I experimented with numerology, astrology, regression therapy, encounter groups, accupressure, psychics and Mary Kay Cosmetics. I got in touch with my feelings, found myself, lost myself, had learning experiences, got centered, cocooned, healed myself, found metaphysical strength in crystals and had out-of-body experiences with oat bran.

I rediscovered the comfort of mashed potatoes and orange Jell-O, recouped the ability to tell my mother how I really am instead of trying to spare her feelings, and I once again experienced the joy of having children in the family. I know I hate cute messages on answering machines, politicians with no class who do lottery ads, and service people who say they'll either be there in the a.m. or the p.m.

I love Charles Kuralt, rap music and the freedom of being on my own, and I miss *Spencer For Hire*, Peter Sellers and Freddy Mercury. My faith in justice was restored when Jim Bakker and Zsa Zsa Gabor took the fall, and my hope for Louisville's future was restored when Jerry Abramson took office.

During the 80's I lost four close friends ranging in age from 36 to 42—one to leukemia, one to a heart attack and two to AIDS—and each time I learned all over again how short and precious life is, and how important it is to spend as much time as you can doing what you want to do, and spending time with people you really care about. I also lost two friends to marriage—a different grief, but grief nonetheless.

I've learned that I'm glad I can still be disillusioned in people, and in love, because it proves to me that I continue to start out basically optimistic and non-cynical about both. I also learned, after a story in the paper, that it is unlawful in Kentucky to handle snakes in religious ceremonies (although I think it's okay to take them out on dates, at least in Indiana).

I've observed that men and women still interact like creatures from alien galaxies: Men went from macho to sensitive and then to schizophrenic; women went from the fast track to the mommy track while some, like me, went off the track altogether.

During the 80's the goal-oriented over-achiever in me grew and prospered, but when it comes to matters of the heart, I learned that peanut butter sometimes has more staying power than broad shoulders and narrow hips.

I've come to appreciate my best friends more than anything because they never say I told you so, and they never remind me of my limitations, only my potential. They bring chocolate and hugs when my heart is broken, and they give sensitive, thoughtful advice: "ARE YOU CRAZY? Lose that guy! What did he ever do to deserve you, anyway?"

They pick me up at the airport in the middle of the night, give me garage space for my car, yell at me, call from London just to see how I'm doing and to say I love you, worry about me when I'm sick, laugh at me when I get on my high horse, come to the hospital to comfort me when a member of my family is seriously ill, argue with me and love me. The best thing about best friends is that they endure—through everything—and they know, as I do, that we're in for the long haul together and that means being there no matter what.

Overall, I think I'm better prepared for the 90's than I was for the 80's. In any case, I'll approach this decade bearing two things in mind. One is my favorite Zen quotation: "In whatever you do, burn yourself like a good bonfire, leaving no trace." The other is what my friend Art says to me when I take myself too seriously: "You would want to get over it."

The Meaning Of Life

My friend Mike rushed into my house last Saturday morning and said, "Excuse me—can you tell me the meaning of life?"

I looked up from the pool table and said, "Well, gee, Mike, I'm kind of busy right now. Can I get back to you?"

"Come on," he insisted. "I'm in a hurry. I've got to drop my date off at the day care center, and I'm a little low on automatic weapons, so I've got to go shopping, and ..."

"Okay, okay," I said, lining up the four ball for the corner pocket. "Write this on your date's Big Chief tablet: Woody Allen said showing up is 80 percent of life, and writer Edward Abbey said, "What is the truth? I don't know, and I'm sorry I brought it up."

"Me, too," Mike said, peering over my shoulder. "By the way, that's a dead scratch if you don't use low English to stop the cue ball. I've told you a thousand times that the purpose of English is to put your cue ball where you want it for the next shot."

As he talked, the four ball clicked neatly in the corner pocket; the cue ball hesitated for a moment, then raced to join the four. I moved around the table to look him in the eye. "Why this sudden need to know the meaning of life?" I asked. "You've never shown any interest in the subject before. The only philosophical view you've ever held is any one that can be summed up on a T-shirt."

"Just what I'd expect from someone who learned Spanish watching Speedy Gonzales cartoons," Mike said. "It's just that I didn't get much satisfaction from the last .44 Magnum I bought, and I began to wonder if I was missing something."

"You're going to be missing a couple of fingers if you don't stop moving the cue ball against the rail," I said. "Why should you be the one to know the meaning of life? Why can't you just show up 80 percent of the time like the rest of us? Or why don't you subscribe to Jack Kerouac's point of view: 'I don't know. I don't care. And it doesn't make any difference'? Or how about Will Durant's: 'As we acquire more knowledge, things do not become more comprehensible, but more mysterious'? Or…"

"Oh, shut up," Mike said as he rearranged the balls. "When you get so cerebral, I just want to slap you. There—you'll never make this shot, either." Satisfied that the five ball was out of reach to all except Minnesota Fats, Mike nodded his head toward the speakers and asked, "Who is that?"

"Steely Dan."

"Steely Dan? I thought he was an aerobics instructor."

"I'm sure you did," I said. "You also thought Nietzsche was a German tractor company. Now take the five ball off the rail and put it back where you found it."

"Jeez, what a grouch. Do you want a beer?" he asked, heading for the kitchen. "Adult conversations require adult beverages."

"You know I never drink beer on Saturday until the cartoons are over," I said, slipping the five ball in the side pocket. "Besides, you could have fooled me that this is an adult conversation."

"I know you cheated while I was in the kitchen," Mike said as he tucked the five ball behind the eight. "You always do."

"Not true," I said. "The meaning of life is not cheating when your friends are out of the room. By the way, your date is probably old enough to start high school by now."

"Oh. Right. I almost forgot about her." Running for the door, Mike said, "By the way, she thinks Armand Hammer is right about the meaning of life. He says we're here to do good."

I thought that over while I racked the balls. Of course, I thought. I should do as much good as I can. And I should put as much paint as I can on the canvas before me, and I should also remember the words of O.J. Simpson: "Thinking is what gets you caught from behind."

All The News That Fits

The other day my friend Jo Ella introduced me to a college friend of hers in a restaurant. We shook hands and I said, "How are you?" His eyes glazed over and he said, "Naps are good for you. Hispanics are not the primary recipients of welfare. Jane Curtin can't stay up late enough anymore to watch Saturday Night Live. There's a new book just out listing all the new books just out. Hank Williams Jr. needs a love doctor. If a wind reaches 74 mph, it is called a hurricane. There's a new performance artist downtown who does 'Skin is Your Largest Organ'…"

Jo Ella stood up abruptly and led her friend back to his table. She returned with a worried look on her face. "He was perfectly okay when I last saw him at Woodstock," she said. "Maybe he's having a psychedelic flashback. What do you think?"

"I think it's clearly a case of Synopsis Syndrome," I said. "Everyone I know in New York has it, but this is the first time I've seen it in Louisville."

"Is this a new social…"

"No, it isn't," I interrupted. "Synopsis Syndrome is a

media-culture-transmitted disease affecting people who are compelled to be abreast of everything. The amount of information available to us doubles every five years, and these people are frantically trying to stay on top of everything. So they get sound bites from TV news, catch *Morning Edition* between snooze alarms, read newspaper headlines, read reviews but never read a book or rarely see the movie, scan magazines, buzz through the cable channels and nod knowingly when someone mentions a new club or art gallery even though they've never heard of it. In other words, these people indiscriminately cram their heads full of information that has been shortened, condensed, headlined, summarized, pulverized, digested, abbreviated, synopsized..."

"Obviously you don't know the meaning of the word synopsis," Jo Ella said, making no effort to hide a wide yawn.

"You should talk, Jo Ella. You're the only person I know who feels compelled to know nothing. You quit reading newspapers because you got ink on your hands, you gave up TV when you found out remote control was not voice-activated, and you stopped reading books because they made your arms tired."

"Stop it. I did not have a problem with the remote control; I just occasionally got it confused with the garage-door opener. Anyway, what happens to people who get Synopsis Syndrome? Do they suffer an abbreviated illness followed by sudden death?"

"Very funny. Actually, the only cure is total information deprivation for a period of six months. When the patient no longer has any idea what's going on in the world— knows of no new books, movies, plays, art galleries, clubs or trends, and can't remember whether this season's hottest item is jeweled flats or overalls—then he is cured. He can then start ingesting information gradually, a paragraph at a time, until he works his way up to reading an entire book. Because the treatment requires no capsulizing or summarizing, the recovery rate is very poor."

"So what happens to those who can't be cured?" Jo Ella asked, idly drawing a truck driver on the tablecloth.

"That's the worst part," I said. "Untreated, Synopsis Syndrome is like the Kudzu vine; it overtakes everything in the victim's life. Everything is reduced to its lowest common denominator. Like your friend, Synopsis Syndrome sufferers regurgitate bits of useless, unrelated information all day long. Over time, they eat smaller and smaller portions at mealtimes, until one day they're down to eating nothing but consommé cubes and drinking evaporated milk. Trying to have a relationship with these people is hopeless...uh oh, your friend is back."

"Jo Ella," he said, "after graduation, I got married. I got divorced. I got married again. I got divorced again. I may be a slow learner, but I don't think this is going to work out for us, either, so I want you to see other people."

Father Knows Best

A few days ago, when I was wallowing in the post-holiday depression that always accompanies the post-holiday bills, I came across a quote attributed to French poet Paul Claudel: "In the little moment that remains to us between the crisis and the catastrophe, we might as well take a glass of champagne."

Now that's news I can use.

I love news I can use, especially when it involves a glass of champagne. The vaccinating effect of a single glass of champagne is far more rewarding between the crisis and the catastrophe than reminding myself that it's always darkest before the dawn, or sweet are the uses of adversity. I'm far more motivated by upbeat pick-me-ups like "I feel so much better now that I've given up all hope," or Marion Smith's reminder that "One of the advantages of living alone is that you don't have to wake up in the arms of a loved one."

Anyway, at about the same time Paul suggested that I have a glass of champagne, I opened a letter from a woman I'd never heard of who also said she had news I could use. She said her message was Urgent and Very Personal. She was having Visions about me, and she wanted to know if I was Feeling All Right. She also thought I was worried about something Very Personal and Very Private, and she felt Something Big was about to happen to me.

I felt certain I was about to be attacked by Capital Letters, but she seemed to think it was far more Personal than that. She was so Concerned, in fact, that she had to stop typing her letter and write me a Personal Note (in Purple Ink) because she was Getting A Feeling Right This Second that a Major Change was about to Happen to me.

Outstanding, I thought, this calls for Another Glass of Champagne! But no, enough about me, she said, and abruptly launched into detail about her background: she lives in Las Vegas now and she said she'd had "Feelings" since she was a child. So have I, I thought, but I've never felt compelled to write to strangers about my "Feelings."

She then listed all her celebrity credentials as an astro-parapsychologist, although she never quite explained what that is. I thought she was a psychologist for space parachutes, but, as it turns out, she is a "sensitive," a visionary, a soothsayer, a fortune teller, a psychic, a Doodah.

I couldn't help but notice that much of her resume was written in the past tense. She said she had been featured on the Maury Povich show (I think she followed the man who grew watermelons on his chest), and she had written a column, and she had done a talk show, and she had done personal forecasts for people far too famous to mention.

I also couldn't help but notice that none of her credentials appeared in Capital Letters.

But then, she said, Enough About Me. Let's get Back To You.

YESSS! I thought, wondering who emptied the champagne bottle. It's about time. WHAT ABOUT ME? WHAT MAJOR CHANGE IS ABOUT TO HAPPEN IN MY LIFE? When will I be rich? When will I be famous? Will I ever want a kitchen stove that actually works? Will I be able to afford Another Bottle of Champagne? Will I have to start using CHAMPAGNE HELPER OR WHAT?

Don't Worry, she purred in the next paragraph, I Will Help You. I just need Something Personal of yours so I can get Closer to You. Something that I can keep. All you have to do is send me a Lock of Your Precious Hair and Your Signature on a Check for $20.

Suddenly I began to get a Vision of my own. It was fuzzy at first, but slowly it began to come into focus. I saw myself as a wide-eyed, golden-haired child sitting spellbound on my father's knee. He was patiently explaining life's eternal verities to me:

"When you grow up, my child, there are certain things you can always count on. First of all, MTV will be invented after you grow up, and the first person you will always see when you turn on MTV is Brian Adams. Even when Brian Adams is 100 years old, he'll still be on MTV.

"Another thing that will always happen is this: no matter where you live, there will always be a house in the neighborhood with Neighbors So Quiet that you will never see nor hear them. Pay attention to this house, because one morning you will pick up the newspaper and read this headline: EXTREMELY QUIET NEIGHBORS RUN AMOK WITH CHAIN SAW."

"And, the last thing that you can always count on is this: Fools will always be parted from their money, but it will be a lot less painful if you have a glass of champagne before you write the check."

Don't Worry, Be Happy

Not long ago I read an article which outlined seven ways to cure the blues. I was feeling pretty good at the time, but I read it anyway. Since Geminis are the mood rings of the Zodiac, I never know from minute to minute if I'm going to be on the sweet end of an endorphin rush or if I'll be browsing through the new best seller, *Final Exit*.

Most of what I learned in this article wasn't new—make yourself feel better by exercising, listening to music, connecting with other people and seeking out a professional. I really like that—"seek out a professional." A professional what? Hit man? Blues singer? Anyway, the author also suggested that eating right would make you feel better.

I like that, too. It made me reflect on the times in my life when I've felt really bad, and I wondered if I would have enjoyed my divorce more if I'd had a good meal. In the middle of the very next crisis I have, I'm going to excuse myself and go wolf down some kelp and tree bark.

The theory is, of course, that eating right stabilizes your blood sugar. If you're feeling low or depressed, then the last thing you want is the highs and lows caused by sugar, alcohol or caffeine. Now that really depressed me. Add nicotine, and you've wiped out my entire food group. My own blood sugar is so destabilized by chocolate and caffeine that it should go to support group meetings twice a week.

But the one item in the article that really got my attention was this: You'll feel better if you make a list of all the things that worry you or make you feel bad—the idea being that a list provides distance from your problems, and allows you to gain some perspective.

Since I'm always in the market for distance and perspective, and since making lists is a great way to avoid actually doing anything productive, I decided to try it out. I skipped the imponderables like nuclear war, the President's language thing and male-female relationships, but here's a couple of other things I worry about:

Since statistics prove that death strikes one out of one, I do worry about death. No doubt about it, death definitely gives me the blues. I don't worry about my own death, but there's a whole long list of people and animals that I don't want to die. However, given that the good die young, I don't worry too much about having to give up my cat, Badman Trouble.

Death worries me for another reason. Whenever I see a flooded disaster area on the news, I always think about the graveyards, and I'm always afraid all those caskets will float up and go cruising around looking for a new home. What could be worse than suffering through a flood and then, once the water's settled, come home to find Zebediah McHamish, circa 1897, hanging out on your doorstep?

Another thing that worries me is the telephone company. I'm certain I'll be punished because I have consistently refused to have casual long distance relationships with any number of carriers, and I have consistently refused to upgrade, modernize or futurize my phone systems beyond the say hello, say goodbye stage. I don't want to know who called last, or who's going to call next, nor do I want to talk to strangers in Omaha just because they have the same phone system I have.

So here's what I worry about. Someday, the phone company will flip a magic switch and all of my telephone conversations will be broadcast on the radio in my mother's kitchen. Shortly after she's overheard me suggesting helpful things to do with the latest product or service someone tried to sell me on the telephone, she will call me up and say "You want something to worry about? I'll give you something to worry about."

Life Is Just A Lottery

I had a dream the other night, and like most of my dreams, it was in black and white highlighted with hot-pink neon. Maybe it's because I watch too much MTV, or maybe because I ate anchovy pizza before I went to bed. Anyway, Governor Lotto appeared before me, in black and white, told me I had just won a million dollars in the Kentucky Lottery, handed me a hot-pink neon check and demanded to know what I was going to do with the money.

It is the only question Governor Lotto has ever asked that I've found interesting, so instead of shouting, "Spend it!," I gave the answer considerable thought.

I don't think I should feel guilty that my first impulse was to buy my car a garage, but I somehow felt this money had been given to me for a higher purpose, particularly since I didn't buy a lottery ticket.

It seemed to me, after careful consideration, that the best options for the lottery money would be to set up several new lotteries that would enable everyone to participate without spending money they would otherwise spend on life's necessities—food, shelter, pantyhose and

Moosehead.

In the "Two for One Emotional Disorder Dream-stakes," for example, you could trade in non-referential anxiety and repressed feelings for fear of sophisticated kitchen gadgetry from the Williams Sonoma catalog; or you could exchange fear of failure and low self-esteem for the Donald Trump or D. Wayne Lukas ego ideal.

In the final grand-prize round, emotional shut-ins who have a fear of commitment would get one chance in a lifetime to become a Love Slave.

The price of an 'Emotional Dreamstakes' ticket would be getting in touch with your feelings, and the odds of acquiring an emotional disorder worse than what you have would be about one in five.

If you're attached to your old emotional insecurities and wouldn't choose to trade them in, you could play 'Relationship Rub-Off,' the lottery for couples who want to correct their dysfunctional behavior in a mature manner.

For instance, if you rubbed off the two spots on the ticket and revealed the words *jealous* and *possessive,* you would receive these instructions: "If you love something, let it go free. If it does not come back, it was never meant to be yours. But if it does, punish it forever." Or: "Jealousy and possessiveness are indications that you don't trust your partner. Don't live with doubt and insecurity. Hire a private detective and confront your lover with hard evidence—then sue."

If the rub-off spots revealed the words *needy* and *dependent,* you'd be advised to remind your lover that you didn't take him/her to wet-nurse, and suggest that he/she find someone else to lean on.

The price of a 'Relationship Rub-Off' ticket would be

your unwillingness to accept the blame for anything, and the odds would be about one in three that you'd make your relationship even worse than it already is.

With your emotional problems solved, and knowing that you no longer had to waste time working on your relationship, you could concentrate on the biggest dream game of all—'The Guess-Where-the-Kentucky-Lottery-Money-Goes Sweepstakes.'

In order to win the first level of play, you'd take a one-step multiple-choice exam: "The Kentucky Lottery Money Goes to..."

A. The Department of Health, Human Resources and Relocation of Politicians.

B. The Department of Transportation, Special Division: Stretch Toyotas.

C. The Bureau of Law Enforcement, Special Forces: Cab Driver Sneaker Inspector.

D. The Commission To Prove That Abraham Lincoln Never Set Foot in Indiana.

E. All of the above.

If you chose "All of the above," you'd qualify for the random drawing for the grand prize—an autographed picture of Governor Lotto surrounded by hopeful school children.

A Message
From The Void

My good friend DooDah, psychic guru and paperhanger, is whiling away his hours in the Big House after being snagged for perfecting a new $10,000 bill. Since DooDah has a lot of time on his hands, he recently sent me a long letter that I'd like to share with you:

"Despite the fact that some of my favorite entreprencurial endeavors have been sharply curtailed, prison is not all bad. While the quality of the leather we are given to work with is not up to your standards, the wallets are quite nice and I'll send you two dozen or so for Christmas presents. Please deposit the usual sum in my account in Geneva and tell them I'll be around in three-to-five to collect.

"Since I haven't heard from you since the end of July, I suspect you've been engaged in something that is beyond your control, but we will deal with matters of the heart in good time. You know, of course, that I always know what is on your mind even if you don't communicate with me directly, and I understand your reluctance to visit me again since one of my roommates has been planning his escape with you in mind.

"But not to worry. Inner peace is at hand because I have the answers you seek:

"God was not trying to punish you by giving you curly hair. She was only trying to save you a lifetime of the cost of perms. She did, however, think you'd have the good sense to live in a city whose major tourist attraction was something other than a summer-long humidity festival. She seemed a little miffed that She only hears from you when you're in trouble (upon reflection, She decided that She hears from you quite enough). She did suggest you might threaten your hair with a cattle prod and a stronger gel. She'll be in touch.

"I know that your cat Miscellaneous went blind in July. The next time someone gently suggests that Mizzie might be better off if—well, you know, you shouldn't get upset and shout, "If your mother went blind, would you have her put to sleep?" People mean well, so just tell them that she's in no pain, she's still purring and you're certain she'd far prefer occasionally bumping into a wall over being dead.

"I've told you time and time again that taking your car to the VET is not voluntary. That notice has been lying on your kitchen table for three weeks and it says there's a bench warrant out for your arrest. I don't think they're kidding.

"You too often associate existentialism with Sartre and Camus; existentialism was actually fully outlined by Kierkegaard, who suggested that life is short and limited in space and time. Therefore it is necessary to leap fearlessly into the void with complete commitment to the unknown, willing to risk the self utterly and accept the fact that within your lifetime there probably will never be any heavy-metal chamber music.

"Continue your search for the meaning of life, recognizing that...

– life is complex, but you should not measure your life by the breath you take, but by its breathtaking moments;

– the lottery, which is gambling for people who've lost the will to live, will never pay for first-class education;

– when friends get married, they often cease to be your friends because they don't understand that marriage should make the circle larger, not smaller;

– you're one of only two people who thought *Blue Velvet* was a funny movie;

– infatuation is temporary insanity, but you may discover that it is possible to love someone until the day you die;

– you must protect your ears when you go hear The Hammerheads;

– the new HerpAquarium is not an exhibit for social disease;

– you can tell if a mole is suspicious when he won't look you in the eye;

– that which does not kill us makes us stronger;

– most personal problems can be solved with a suitable application of high explosives."

I could almost hear DooDah sigh in conclusion: "Write when you find work, and let me know if you need money."

I thought you should know.

It's My Party
And I'll Cry If I Want To

I was helping my friend Leapo clean up the party afterbirth following his annual New Year's Eve 'Come as Others See You' bash when I noticed he had tears in his eyes.

"Why are crying?" I asked. "Is it because only three people came to the party? Maybe you ought to change the theme. You've been doing this for years and no one can ever figure out what to do. When you ask people to present themselves as others see them, who has the courage to come to a party as an insensitive bore, or a raging egotist, or a knee-jerk liberal or a…"

"Well, you for one," Leapo said. "Anyway, it's supposed to be a joke. Maybe I just don't know anyone with a sense of humor, or maybe they all went to Walter's 'Year in Review' party. Personally, I don't see what's so festive about starting the new year dressed up as a dirty Boston Harbor or as a person who died of boredom after watching the entire 30 hours of *War and Remembrance*.

"Anyway," he concluded, dumping eight pounds of Cheese Whiz Wonder Bread sandwiches in the trash can, "I'm not crying. And if I were it wouldn't be because the people who did come thought I was representing a bad host who serves food from the 50's.

"But maybe you're right about the theme," he went on. "It was pretty depressing bringing in the New Year with a Dan Quayle replicate who thinks polled Herefords are cows who participate in public-opinion surveys. And his wife..."

"Look, Leapo," I said, "Theme parties are out anyway. Why don't you just have a regular old New Year's Eve party next year with whistles and horns and funny hats and that bubbly stuff that makes people so stupid they wish they'd gone to a party in a foreign country?

"Or have a simple Derby party this spring with a betting pool and a few gallons of that horrible sticky brown stuff that we're so famous for. It's hard enough to just get through the day. Why does every party have to challenge people to stretch the limits of their imagination and creativity?"

"Well, aren't you the unimaginative one?" Leapo said, scraping out a tub of lime-green Jell-O in the trash can. "But what could I expect from someone whose idea of a good party is simply that the cops don't show up? Listen, do you think your dog would eat this?" he asked, staring at four cafeteria trays filled with meatloaf.

"I resent that comment about the cops," I said. "Although I admit it is more relaxing to have a party without them. Actually, I think the best party has three components—a six-pack, a pizza and the U of L Cardinals. I also think my dog would call the Humane Society if I brought that meatloaf home."

"Okay," Leapo said. "Let's see what it takes to challenge your imagination. Let's assume for a moment that you had to have a party without basketball, a pool game, Aretha Franklin, David Allan Coe or Bob Schulman playing the drums. What would you do?"

"I'd declare that life wasn't worth living, I guess. No, wait. I've got it. How about a party for smokers with biblical names all starting with the letter 'B'? What do you want to do with these, Leapo?" I asked, holding two giant Tupperware bowls of creamed corn poised over the trash can.

"Oh, just dump it," he said. "I know your dog won't eat yellow food, and creamed corn makes my garbage disposal throw up. And stop calling me Leapo. You know I hate that. It's Leopold, LEO-POLD."

"But don't throw those away," Leapo shouted, pointing to two coolers filled with mashed potatoes. "I'll freeze them and on Valentine's Day I'll have a 'Potatoes on Parade' party. Everyone could bring a potato dish. You know, potato pancakes cut into heart shapes and sweet potatoes for your sweetheart."

"That's a great idea," I said. "And we can invite all the smokers with biblical 'B' names. Let's see, there's Barabbas Harding and Bathsheba Swann and Benjamin Jackson and Boaz Miller and…"

Woman With No Broom

Woman With No Broom

One day last summer after my bank and I had decided to remodel my kitchen and bedroom, the carpenter and I stood in the kitchen discussing the layout for the new cabinets. He said that the cabinet at the end of the counter should be tall enough to hold a broom.

"That would be nice," I agreed. "But I don't own a broom."

His eyes closed momentarily; then the conversation continued. We decided that the tall cabinet could contain dog food, cat food and gourmet items such as pork and beans and warm six-packs.

A few minutes later a worried look crossed his face and he asked, "You don't own a broom? I've never known a woman who didn't own a broom. How do you clean your floors?"

He was trying very hard to work out this mysterious equation—solving for clean if x is the broom.

"It's easy," I said. "Once a week people who have brooms come here and use them and I pay them money."

"Oh," he said. "That costs a lot of money, doesn't it?"

"It depends on how you look at it," I said. "You see,

most people work so they can have money to do things. I work so I can not do some things. Like cleaning floors. It's like the government pays people not to grow soybeans. I get no psychic reward from cleaning floors. I get psychic reward from not cleaning floors."

He didn't appear to understand, so I pressed on.

"See, these people who come here with brooms went into business to clean floors. So they must like it. So they get to do what they like—clean floors—and I get to do what I like—which is not cleaning floors."

"Is it because you don't have a husband?" he asked suspiciously—still solving for x.

"No, that has nothing to do with it," I answered. "I used to have one of those and I still got no satisfaction from cleaning. If he had liked cleaning, then fine, he could have done it. But the idea of sparkling blue toilet bowl water and no waxy build-up just has no appeal. It may be a man's world, but I don't have to clean it. So the fact that the end cabinet will be tall enough to hold a broom is interesting, but irrelevant.

"Think of it this way," I continued, as he glanced furtively at the door. "A lot of people work so they can travel, or buy fine clothes or jewelry, or keep the refrigerator full of designer water. I work so that I don't have to do my own 15,000-mile checkups, fix my roof or learn how to stretch hamburger 101 ways. When I give people money, they change my oil and check my battery, put shingles on my house, give me a brand new completely unstretched hamburger, and more importantly, they scrub the toilet and sweep the floors."

"Still," he said, shaking his head slowly, "I just don't know about a woman who don't own a broom."

The Corroding 4x4 Blues

I n the bottom of my desk drawer, under my bronzed baby-food dish and a yellowed letter from my high school principal refusing my mother's attempts at plea-bargaining, I have a list called 'Things I Should Never Ever Do Under Any Circumstances, No Matter What.'

It's an old list that's gone through countless revisions, and it includes reminders to stop dating after I get married, never be rude to the IRS and never buy a used car.

So far I've managed to stop short before actually doing any of these things—except, of course, for the most destructive one: I bought a used car. Worse, I bought a used truck.

I have a perfectly good car, but I perceived the need to have a second car. Something large enough to transport more than me and half a passenger. A truck, of course!

A truck, I thought, would be impervious to dirt, dog slobber and hit-and-run drivers.

A truck would love ice and snow, and it would be so anonymous that I could park anywhere and not be noticed. The truck would be so unattractive, too, that I could leave the windows down and the motor running;

thieves would sneer and leave notes on the windshield: "Dream on, Sucker."

My dad thought the truck was a good idea as long as I didn't get a four-wheel-drive. You don't need it, he said, and a four-wheel-drive is more expensive to keep up and repair. My dad is a smart man.

I was still holding on to that thought when I went to see a 1978 4X4 Chevy Blazer advertised in The Bargain Mart. It's just for fun, I said to myself. I wasn't even sure what a Chevy Blazer looked like.

Finding the owner's house was easy. Bigfoot sat in the driveway, fully visible a mile away. Up close it looked clean, appealing and rust-free. It was also considerably larger than my first apartment.

The test drive was exhilarating. I could look eye-to-eye with TARC drivers, I could see over every car in the street, and I could haul around the entire cast of *Deliverance* if I felt like it. I was satisfied that the Blazer's only shortcoming was its uncompromising Wildcat colors—blue and white. That's easy to fix, I thought. Instead of the usual 'Get It Up' plate found on the front of most 4X4's, I'd get a tasteful version of a Cardinal choking the living daylights out of a Wildcat.

I wrote the check and drove home wondering if the radio would pick up anything other than WAMZ.

I love the Blazer. A blue and white behemoth is far from anonymous, but it's fun to drive, the air-conditioner is cold enough to cure meat, and it does satisfy some of the practical needs I'd conjured up. Ten years ago, it was best of breed. But its pedigree, I quickly found out, is a little rusty.

For example, I knew the door on the driver's side was

almost impossible to close unless you run at it full speed and hit it with your shoulder. And so what if the glass in the tailgate gets off track a little? And who cares if the upholstery rips your stockings to shreds? People who drive 4X4's shouldn't be wearing stockings anyway. Or skirts for that matter.

But I wasn't expecting to have to replace the flywheel. Not the starter motor, a simpler and less expensive proposition, but the flywheel, which meant the entire transmission had to come out. My dad's words flashed like neon in my brain: IT WILL BE MORE EXPENSIVE TO REPAIR.

Then I discovered the glass in the tailgate gets off track because there is no track on one side; it has rusted away and must be replaced. Ed, of Hugh & Ed's Auto Service, who is now a close personal friend and trusted ally, explains rust to me. Rust, I thought, was something you can see and feel. And since I didn't see any, I vaulted to the conclusion that there wasn't any. Not so, Ed says. Rust is the equivalent of 'truck termites,' silently eating through the inside and underside, leaving trails of tears and iron oxide all over my checkbook.

The bad door on the driver's side suffers from the same problem. It does not need a simple hinge. It needs to be replaced because the House of Rust has opened up a new showroom inside the door.

I mention the previous owner to Ed in the context of several illegal and shockingly violent acts. Ed dissuades me. I am now a good customer and Ed has grown accustomed to seeing me several times a week. Ed does not wish to see me go to prison where the bars never rust.

Perhaps I'll just satisfy my impulse for retribution by

sending the previous owner a Neil Young album. An album that could only be written by someone who owned a 1978 Chevy Blazer. An album entitled *Rust Never Sleeps*.

Strangers In Produce

Just when I thought supermarkets were the only safe place left to go, an ugly national trend has presented itself right here in River City: supermarket singles nights.

Is nothing sacred? Up to now, supermarkets welcomed people like me—hungry, ill-tempered and unattractively attired. Even men could go to supermarkets with their hair in curlers. The supermarket was a place where people could safely release their hostilities by cart-banging and line-jumping and express-lane-lying and snatching produce away from old people. It was all good clean fun.

Even the supermarket employees could be counted on to do their part. They would cheerfully bruise out-of-season produce that costs the per-ounce equivalent of a new gold coin and snarl at you if you tried to sneak expired coupons by them and punish you by putting a 25-pound bag of dog food on top of the eggs. The express-lane checker could always be counted on to scream at the top of her lungs, "YOU LIAR! YOU'VE GOT ELEVEN ITEMS. SOMEBODY CALL THE COPS!"

It was great. Everyone knew what to expect from a

grocery-shopping trip.

Now that this despicable trend of supermarket singles-mingling has appeared locally, those of us who only go grocery shopping when we're tired and cranky and visually unappealing are out of luck. Just the thought of having to go grocery shopping in the first place puts me in a bad mood. The thought of having something other than my groceries checked out makes me very mean.

Frankly, though, I don't hold out much hope that this fad will pass quickly, since one supermarket in the East reported its singles night attracted over 2,000 customers.

"How bad can a supermarket singles night be?" I'm sure you're asking. In my worst fantasy, here's how bad it can be:

I need seven cans of dog food, a can of tuna, a six-pack and a bag of bridge mix—a list carefully designed to cover the four basic food groups and get me through the express lane without lying. I roar into the parking lot, full of determination to break my all-time record for minimum time elapsed in a supermarket (four minutes, 39 seconds) and encounter TWO THOUSAND SINGLE PEOPLE. And worse, they're all DRESSED UP. Oh, say it ain't so.

My time elapsed for the four basic food groups is three hours, 14 minutes and eight seconds. And what happens during this three hours, 14 minutes and eight seconds? Do I have a good time? No, I do not. My little heart is black and full of the unspeakable acts I wish to perpetrate upon the architect of this horrible notion of singles mingling among the meat and mangoes.

During this seemingly endless stretch of time I have been asked to participate in the Spandex Singalong in aisle one. Whoever knows all the words to "You're My

New Disease But Don't Spread Yourself Around" will win an antique disco glitter-ball left over from the 70's, when singles met where God intended them to meet—in dark sleazy bars full of poisonous polyester and hairspray fumes.

While I wrestle for my dog food, not to mention my honor, the butcher-turned-deejay makes the following announcement: "Attention, single shoppers. The next blue-light special, Bowling for Dates, is about to begin in aisle two. Would 10 single shoppers please arrange themselves in a pyramid at the end of the aisle? Cantalopes have been provided for your bowling pleasure, but the management must point out that purchase is required."

Meanwhile, in aisle three, where my lone can of tuna resides, 300 men and women are taking advantage of a free aerobics class, taught by the woman who used to scream "LIAR!" at me in the express lane. I barely recognize her now, all done up in smiles and fairly bursting her neon Spandex leotard with good health and designer-water sweat.

Finally, in aisle eight, as I lurch toward the check-out lane, The Shopping Cart Police are making random checks to determine whether shoppers' selections pass upscale yuppie standards. I'm cited for N.C. (no caviar), N.B. (no Brie), and fined an extra $10 for being caught with a half-empty six-pack.

And when the Wardrobe Police show up, I'm cited for vagrancy.

Mess? What Mess?

Recently, while I was beavering away over my cranky computer keyboard, I was interrupted by loud scrabbling noises behind me. I turned to find my neighbor burrowing her way through stacks of papers, books, magazines, coffee cups, ashtrays, empty pizza boxes and the brittle corpse of a poinsettia plant that arrived during the 1988 Christmas holidays.

"Good morning," Jessica said, finally emerging into view. Her smiling face was framed by a complete collection of 1989 *Wall Street Journals*.

"Good morning to you," I said, eyeing a stack of swaying coffee cups threatening to commit suicide. "Whatever you do," I said, "don't move."

"Don't worry," she said, backing out slowly. "I just wanted to say hi because I haven't seen anything except the top of your head for months. I hope you have a fire extinguisher buried under there somewhere."

I held my breath as the coffee cups picked up momentum and the newspapers began to tremble. When Jessica reached the doorway, she turned and said, "By the way, tomorrow is Clean Desk Day."

"Thank you so much for your support," I called after her. But I'm sure she didn't hear me since the crash that followed probably sent Iben Browning rushing out to declare that his earthquake predictions were right all along.

I can't help it. The soft siren song of "paper and clutter, paper and clutter" is so deeply buried in my DNA that the world's best organization expert would start to keen upon encountering my natural habitat.

And I don't know where the clutter gene came from. Everyone else in my family is neat. My mother said it started when I was a baby; anything I could move or drag or pick up, I put in my crib. I learned to read very early because I flooded the mailbox and the house with all the catalogs, brochures and leaflets that followed the "Check here if you want more information" box. By the time I was five, I had a real good grip on life insurance and the Rosicrucians.

The fact is, I love my clutter and I expect I'll always be surrounded by it unless I'm overtaken by a Virgo or a neatnik robot, but I do have a fear that my house will be ransacked by burglars and I would never know except for this note:

"Dear Occupant,

We are hardened criminals who are wise to all the modern techniques used to fight crime and/or evil, but frankly, your methods of crime-fighting have us baffled. We feel certain that your house contains articles of value somewhere underneath the mountains of books, news-papers, magazines, papers, manuscripts, stacks of coffee cups, empty pizza boxes and smoldering ashtrays, but, according to the priority list of our Organized Crime

Calendar, we simply do not have the time to devote to finding whatever it is you may have.

"We were pleased to note, however, that you do have a fire extinguisher buried underneath every *Esquire* magazine published since 1971. And while we were poking about, we ran across your translation of *War and Peace* as a punk-rock tone poem. Honestly—do you have a day job?

"In case you're interested in a professional tip, you could hire an organization expert to come in here and whip this place into shape and we still wouldn't come back on a bet. In all the days of our long and distinguished criminal careers, we have never encountered an animal more vicious than your cat.

"Your dog (at least we think it is a dog) seemed to know that we weren't going to accomplish anything, so he went back to watching TV. It was clever of you, however, to choose both animals in gray and white; they really blend in well with all the newspapers. In fact, the only time we got a really good look at the cat was when he leapt onto Spike's face.

"Well, we have places to go and things to move, but at least this wasn't a complete loss. Spike discovered he was wiping the blood off his face with a pair of underwear, size 34, which should fit him perfectly. Shame on you! I'm going to tell your mother. Sincerely, Vinnie."

Sure enough, Mom called the other night and said, "I hear there's a new man in your life. Who is he? Where did you meet him? How's it going? Hello? I said how's it going?"

"It's, uh, kind of hard to say how it's going, Mom," I said. "I seem to have misplaced him."

Tips For
Easy Housekeeping

After several unsuccessful attempts to find a corporate CEO position, a good friend of mine announced that he was going to start a housekeeping service. He blamed his failure to land the job of choice on his resume: 10 years as a bounty hunter (with no bounty to show for it) and six months driving around one of those trucks full of extremely clean tools.

I blamed his failure to find the job of choice on the fact that he showed up for job interviews wearing T-shirts emblazoned with mottoes like 'It's Never Too Late to Have a Happy Childhood' or 'I Wish You Were a Beer.' I pointed out that most corporate dwellers don't appreciate such cheerful insouciance, but he was determined to DO IT HIS WAY. In fact, his favorite T-shirt heralds the fact that he may be doing nothing, but he's doing it HIS way.

At any rate, he's now a little concerned that his lack of housekeeping experience will stand between him and a six-figure income. I reminded him that a double digit income would be an improvement; nonetheless, I agreed to give him some housekeeping tips since, as he said, I live in a house and therefore must know how to keep one.

How To Keep House:

• Tell the homeowner that you will come in once a week and remove dirt (dirt is anything that is visible at 10 feet and can't be eaten or sat upon; it only exists on floors, unless the homeowner owns teen-agers, in which case you are wasting your valuable time). Dirt is removed with a large noisy implement with a hose attached. It leaves tracks in the carpet. The homeowner likes these tracks because they create the impression that you have actually vacuumed the carpet. When the vacuum no longer picks up large pieces of dirt, it means the vacuum is hopelessly clogged with other large pieces of dirt.

• Tell the homeowner that you will also clean the bathroom. This is very simple. First, flush the toilet. Second, use a can of appliance-white spray paint on the tub and the sink (tip: try to do your cleaning early in the day so the paint dries before the homeowner returns home; otherwise it's hard to explain and could cause a setback in your new career).

• Promise the homeowner that you will be very careful and that you will never break anything. Each week, however, you must break something valuable that was located in an obscure place. This will make the homeowner think you were doing a thorough job. Then pile all the pieces in the middle of the kitchen table and leave a note. Never take the blame for these mishaps. Blame them on cosmic forces; you were just an innocent bystander who could have been killed: "Cabinet door jumped open, antique dish fell out and broke into a jillion pieces. I have decided not to sue, but my attorney insists that you nail all the aforementioned cabinet doors shut immediately."

• Tell the homeowner that under no circumstances will you wash dishes. Otherwise the homeowner will plan a sit-down dinner for 36 people every week before you come. In fact, tell the homeowner that you would prefer he or she didn't eat at all the day before you come because the sight of those crusty dishes with leftover food makes you sick.

• Dusting is easy; be sure to promise the homeowner that you will do some. Before you leave the house, spray a trail of Lemon Pledge in the air behind you. The lingering smell will reassure the homeowner for several weeks. At a later point, say in six to eight months, hold the vacuum-hose thing about 12 inches over every tabletop and it will suck up most of the big dirt. If the homeowner gets picky about the fine gray film over everything else, tell him or her to suck it up.

• Only change the sheets in the guest room, assuming, of course, there have been no guests. If the homeowner asks you to change sheets that have actually been slept in for the last seven days, look aggrieved and let him or her know that you have higher standards than that.

• Do not vacuum or spray paint any pets. It might improve their looks, but it will make the homeowner surly and mean. Instead, bring them toys that you've made yourself out of spools and twine, and leave an occasional note praising them to their owner: "I swear, Ruth Ann is just about the smartest dog/cat/ferret/opossum I've ever seen. Just this morning, while I was painting—I mean cleaning—the bathroom, he/she/it brought in this six-foot garden snake. At least I think it was a garden snake. It had a wedge-shaped copper-colored head and it was real pretty. I left it in the toilet tank for you, but it seems to have disappeared. Oh well, I guess it will turn up somewhere.

Best wishes, your housekeeper.

"P.S. I'm glad you like my work, and I really appreciate the generous tips, profit sharing plan and Christmas bonus, but could you possibly switch your checking account to a bank somewhere in this country?"

Are We There Yet?

The new year is only a month old and I've already had a phone call from my mother asking for a progress report on my New Year's resolutions. Not only was I not surprised—I was prepared: My mother has her own version of the corporate Progress Against Objectives report, and like any good CEO, I know she expects a monthly update.

In order to make the reporting process easier, I had organized my resolutions/objectives by category, and, after being assured that my dad, aka the Chief Financial Officer, was taking his customary mid-morning nap on the couch, I introduced my presentation:

"Madam Chair, in the interest of time and your telephone bill, here is a brief update on the first Progress Against Objectives report for the month of January, 1992, in the following categories: 1. Whining and Moaning; 2. Nutrition; 3. Personal Maintenance; 4. Domestic Skills; and 5. Animal Training."

"Excuse me?" Madam Mom said. "What happened to Personal Relationships, Going To Church, Saving Money and Retail Outlets Who Call The Police If They Even

Think You're Going To Shop There? What happened to Do You Think You Can Fool Your Mother For A Minute, and Have You No Shame? I'm on to your cover-up tactics, so let's just start over. It's pretty obvious you've made no progress in the Do You Think You Can Fool Your Mother For A Minute and Have You No Shame…"

"Not true," I protested. "I've made a lot of progress in Have You No Shame. Just the other day I was overcome with shame when I found an old ABBA Greatest Hits album, and I was deeply ashamed of what I thought when someone gave me one of the monks' fruitcakes for Christmas…"

"That's bush league shame," Mom said. "I don't know who ABBA is, so that doesn't count at all, and fruitcake makes Mother Teresa think bad thoughts, so that doesn't count either. I want some major league shame, something in the Personal Relationships or Going To Church category."

"But, Mom, you promised not to mix up the categories. We agreed in December that the only chance I have to demonstrate progress in some areas is to keep the categories separate…"

"Well, my dear," Mom said. "I see we're not doing too well in the Whining and Moaning category, either, now are we?"

"Okay, fine." I said. "But don't tell me I haven't made some progress in Animal Training. The last time I took Badman Trouble to the vet, he didn't cry. No, Mother, I meant the doctor. The doctor didn't cry, and all but one of his wounds were only superficial. Yes, Mother, the doctor's wounds. And when we left, the receptionist said she thought it all went rather well, and she's decided not to take any legal action due to lingering facial tics she's had ever since Badman's first visit."

"So," I rushed on, sensing I was on a roll for the first time since the conversation started, "You see, I've made good progress in Animal Training, and I also have good news in the Nutrition category. I'm determined to improve my eating habits, and I've made a concentrated effort to expand my food groups beyond fat and caffeine. But the really good news is this: from now on, I'm only going to eat vegetarian desserts."

"And," I said, trying to force closure, "On the Domestic Skills front, the water in the bottom of the fridge is down to about four inches, and I've finally gotten most of the turkey cleaned off the inside of the microwave. You'd think someone would tell you that a turkey explodes if you cook it for two hours on high while it's still in the plastic bag. But no, find out the hard way. Anyway..."

"Never mind," Mother said. "I'd just as soon not be reminded of Christmas dinner; the next time we come to your house for Christmas, I'll bring all the food like I wanted to in the first place. You sounded so confident that I just lost my head; but I do think the rubber display turkey was a nice touch for the table while we were eating tuna sandwiches. But if it ever happens again, please, please for heaven's sake don't make tuna dressing and don't put cranberry sauce on the sandwiches."

"Right, Mom," I said.

Whine, moan. Whine, moan.

Let's Get Organized

The goal-oriented nature of the American work ethic has caused even the most shiftless among us to become compulsively organized. A multi-million dollar industry has mushroomed in the last few years to organize the frenzied overachiever—the type A "where am I right now? what am I doing? where do I go next?" personality.

These organizers are called systems, and they're sold in department stores, drugstores, bookstores and feedstores. They have titles like *How to Organize Yourself in an Early Grave and Where Am I This Nanosecond?*

These systems are used by the same people who pick up the phone on a half-ring, have a follow-up file for the dog and buy cemetery plots upon graduating from high school.

The one thing these organizers all have in common is—aarrgh—the things-to-do-list.

We are consummate listmakers. We make lists; we read books of lists; we read books on how to make lists.

But we could make lists that would solve global problems. Think what could happen if George Bush's list looked like this:

Tell Saddam Hussein he's made my day;
Rambo arrives tomorrow 0800 hours

Tell the S&L's the party's over;
The federal deficit is theirs to pay

Put America back to work

But no. Mr. Bush's list looks like this:

Pick up Barbara's new Adolpho at cleaners

Wash First Dog

Call Bill Clinton and ask him which wine goes
with cheese grits

Put up press conference sign:
"Thank you for not sleeping"

Sometimes the whole world can see the results of one
person's list of things to do today, like Lee Iacocca's:

Borrow some money

Turn Chrysler around

Learn mass-marketing

Most lists are more mundane than that, and most lists
don't solve global problems, but they have destroyed a
major institution in this country—marriage. That's right.

Lists are the major cause of divorce. Take my list of errands for last Saturday morning:

> Call Mom and Dad
>
> Take nap
>
> Go to grocery
>
> Take nap
>
> Pick up cleaning
>
> Take nap

Every item on this list has something in common: each one has a beginning, a middle and an end. Closure. Pick up the phone, write a check for the groceries, hang the clothes in the closet, close eyes, open eyes; these items are history. They're done. Kaput. Finis.

Now see what happens when you have the same list, but with one added item:

> Get married

At first glance it looks okay. You get married, and you cross it off the list. Except it doesn't have closure. It's still there. Day in, day out. It never goes away. And it begins to annoy you. It doesn't lend itself to short-term problem-solving:

> Go to grocery

Take nap

Buy clean underwear

Take nap

Fix marital relationship

It just doesn't work. So the overachievers and the Type A's go quietly berserk for a few years trying to figure out how to get this item off the list. Finally the Aha syndrome occurs.

Aha, we shout, slapping our foreheads, and then the next list looks like this:

Go to grocery

Pick up cleaning

Take nap

Get divorce

Puppy Dearest

It began innocently enough with a card from the veterinary clinic reminding me that it was time for Tori's spring checkup.

When I called for an appointment, I heard a series of low, menacing growls, which I assumed were Tori's, but they belonged to Simone, the receptionist. Simone has had spontaneous hostile reactions to my dog ever since our winter visit when Tori mistook her fuzzy green leg-warmers for a clump of shrubbery.

I had my own anxiety about seeing the vet again, since I was taken to task the last time over Tori's marginal retention of baby fat.

"Ms. McCafferty," the doctor had intoned, "this is not an Akita; this is a polar bear."

"But, doctor," I tried to explain, "he's not overweight; he just has a big frame."

"Maybe so," the doctor replied. "But if you keep adding food to this frame, your dog will owe $5,480 in state road taxes."

When you've been living with a big, hungry, grumpy dog who's been forced to give up pizza, bridge mix, ice cream and hot buttered popcorn from the Vogue, it doesn't help matters any when your vet is located in a fashionable part of town. When Tori and I arrived for our most recent visit, we were met by snickers and jeers from an Afghan, a set of greyhound twins and an impossibly svelte whippet. Tori's social skills are rocky even when he's in a good mood, and I had to promise him lunch at Taxi's Pizza before he'd let go of the whippet's rib cage.

Then we walked resolutely to the desk and presented ourselves to the cruel Simone, who refused to look up. She rifled through the file, found Tori's card and asked him to step on the scale. She turned her head to look at the digital readout. "ONE HUNDRED AND TWENTY POUNDS!" she shrieked. "The doctor WILL NOT BE PLEASED. Perhaps you'd care to have a seat and think about the fitness concerns you'd like to share with the doctor."

Tori and I sat down next to the extremely nervous but impeccably dressed man with the Afghan, who was peering into a compact mirror and adjusting her jeweled collar. "Oh, Marilyn, stop it," the man said. "You're so vain."

"Excuse me?" I said to him. Tori was snarling again.

"Oh, it's Marilyn, my Afghan," he said. "She thinks her collar is too busy for daytime wear." He leaned toward me and whispered, "Confidentially, I'm at my wit's end with this dog. She sneaks out of the house at night to beg doggie bags from people leaving 610 Magnolia; then she lopes over to the St. James Court fountain, and…"

"You mean Marilyn is…"

"That's right," he said, buffing his nails on his trousers. "Binge and purge, binge and purge. Of course, your dog seems to only know the bingeing part." Tori raised his upper lip, presenting all his teeth, and the man said, "Well, excuuuse me. He doesn't have a very good sense of humor, does he?"

Our little chat was interrupted by Simone, who leaned across her desk and said sweetly, "Mrs. Breedblood, you can take Townsend and Tiffany in the first room on the right." The greyhound twins, weighing a total of 41 pounds, floated away into room number one. Then Simone looked directly at me and said loudly, "Ms. McCafferty, you can take your POLAR BEAR into the room on the left."

The dreaded moment was at hand. We were eye to eye with the doctor, who was about to deliver his second I-thought-I-told-you-to-put-this-dog-on-a-diet speech, when suddenly he stopped and looked at Tori. "What's that hanging out of his mouth?" he asked me.

"What? Oh, that." I said innocently. "That's Simone's skirt. I think Tori thought it was too busy for daytime wear."

Did Badman Act Alone?

Middle East politics aside, I know a lot about naked aggression. I see it acted out in my own home every day.

Late last summer, my beloved cat, Miscellaneous, died because she decided she was finally good and ready to—she was 17, or maybe 18 (she was always vague about her age). The trouble is, she was ready and I wasn't; I missed her terribly.

So, on Labor Day weekend, my sister Carol brought me a kitten about the size of a hamster. She hadn't planned to, but she was mesmerized by two cute little boys standing in front of the drugstore with a basket of kittens—free to a good home. She picked a little gray and white and black-striped number with a perfect 'M' on his forehead. It's a McCafferty cat, she thought. It's destiny!

WRONNNG.

I should have named him Mickey or Mouser or Marmaduke because I know that names contribute a great deal to who you are. But no, I named him Badman Trouble.

Badman Trouble, the kitten, is now five months old.

He has the mentality of Ted Bundy.

Badman Trouble—a.k.a. The Bad Seed, The Terminator, The Prince of Darkness, Freddy Krueger—is a one-kitten demolition squad, a fur-bearing Dirty Harry, a Cat Out of Hell. He slices, he dices, he slashes, he trashes, he dances, he prances.

What's worse, he has the feline equivalent of a 280 IQ. He plans, he connives, he manipulates, he strategizes. He masquerades as cute when he wants to be held—so much easier, you see, to shred you that way. He has learned to make the bass drum go boom by flinging himself at it, or by jumping on the foot pedal.

When he's awake, he's like a cat on crack. Then suddenly, he falls comatose into a little heap; gathering strength for the next round.

I've grown accustomed to walking around the house with Badman fastened to my ankle. I've grown accustomed to having my hands and legs bleed. I'm about a quart low now, but the makers of Neosporin are grateful because I've singlehandedly doubled their local market share.

I've become so acclimated to protecting my food that I fear I'll be mistaken for an ex-convict when I eat out. Mizzie, the good cat, only ate on occasion. With Badman, it's only an occasion if he isn't eating. I've never known an animal who loved his groceries more than Badman. I should have named him Kroger.

The first time I took him to the vet he was curled up, asleep, in my hand. When the receptionist said, "Okay, you can bring Badman in now," everyone in the reception area smiled. Then they chuckled. Then they laughed out loud.

Fools. What did they know? For that matter, what did any of us know then? Now people dive under tables and desks when they see us·coming. The last time I was there, the doctor indicated the pointy wisps of hair in Badman's ears. "See that," he said, wiping blood off his hand, "these are wildcat's ears."

No kidding.

But Badman has to contend with at least one superior being in this household—my dog. Badman hasn't figured this out yet, but Tori is actually not a dog at all. Tori is a Zen being simply having a canine experience with a human and a feline. Tori spends most of his time in a reclining position contemplating the nature of the universe and having soul memories of faraway Akita ancestors in the snowy mountains of Japan.

Tori, now 8, has assumed a benevolent-patriarch role with Badman, and dismisses most of his behavior as immature and frivolous. When Badman prances sideways toward Tori, with his back arched, his eyes agleam and his fur abristle, Tori yawns, dispatches him across the room with one swipe of a mighty paw, then goes back to sleep.

But Tori has made one rule unmistakably clear: If you, Badman Trouble, even think about going near my supper dish, I WILL KILL YOU.

Tori believes that acts of naked aggression should not go unpunished.

All I Really Need To Know

Robert Fulghum's book *All I Really Need to Know I Learned in Kindergarten* is still on the paperback bestseller list, as is Suzy Becker's book, *All I Really Need to Know I Learned From My Cat*.

Having all the answers is obviously a great deal easier than I thought it was; nonetheless, it occurred to me that I'd better hurry up and find a definite source of my own since I don't know nearly as much about anything as I should.

I've read Fulghum's book, and it is good to be reminded that we should always say we're sorry if we hurt someone, and we should hold hands when we go into the street together, and everyday we should play some, work some, dance some, sleep some, eat some and paint some.

And I've read Becker's cat book, and it is good to be reminded that we should not swallow our fur.

Somehow, though, these books failed to tell me all I really need to know about anything. I already knew a lot about furballs from watching *"Beauty and the Beast,"* and I do eat/work/play/dance/sleep and read some every day. I thought maybe what I learned in Sunday School would add the definitive note, but the only thing I remember with clarity is that you have to be quiet in church or Baby Jesus will smack you.

I've been studying my dog, Tori, to see if he can tell me all I really need to know. So far, my study has revealed that, in exchange for doing absolutely nothing, Tori gets fed, watered, walked and loved everyday. It's good work if you can get it, but I've never been able to manage it myself. Of course, Tori is a practicing Zen dog; he holds all the secrets to the universe, but he doesn't share.

I've learned more practical lessons from my own cat, Badman Trouble, than I learned from Becker's cat: (1) If you see something you want, take it. And then hide it under the refrigerator. (2) If you want food, jump on someone's face at 5 a.m. (3) If you want to go out, back up six feet and hurl yourself through the screen door. (4) If you stay out all night, clean your fur and look contrite before you come home. (5) If you see something you don't like, terminate with prejudice.

The only problem with learning from Badman is that his worldview is inconsistent with (a) being a decent human being and (b) staying out of jail.

Desperately seeking sources, I consult my psychic friend, Doodah, who is currently tidying up a debt to society by making attractive new license plates in a state-maintained facility. Doodah announced that he was expecting me.

"How did you know I was coming?" I asked, clutching the wire mesh that separated us.

"That's easy," he said, admiring his handiwork on a newly minted license plate. "I always know when you're in trouble. You emit a high-pitched frequency that only dogs and psychics can hear. You are not seeking a definitive source for all you really need to know about anything. That is a trick your head has played on your heart. You know, of course, that we never know all we need to know about anything. In fact, we know very little. In fact, we know nothing. But never mind that; you came here because you seek The Way."

"The Way? The Way where?" I asked. "The Way to what?"

"It is not The Way to anywhere," Doodah said, polishing his license plate briskly. "It is simply The Way. And The Way for you now is to contemplate the words of Robert Frost—'The best way out is always through'."

"I knew that," I said.

"No, you didn't." Doodah said. "But you will. You have much to learn right now, and you will. Trust me."

"Of course," I said. "I trust you completely. But before I go, I think you better take another look at those license plates. I think they're supposed to say "Wander Indiana"—not "Why Indiana."

Smiling Through The Apocalypse

Riding Out The Recession

If it's true that money returns to its rightful owner during a recession, then I'd like to know who the rightful owners are and why they want my money back.

I thought I was doing more than my fair share for the economy—I was out there consuming goods and services right and left just like everyone else. So much so, in fact, that if it's time for me to return my money to its rightful owner, there is very little left to return.

But I'm a fair person, and well, okay, if my money belongs to someone else, I can find out who it belongs to and give it back. So I thought of all those who are in a position to dispense largesse in the first place, and I called them up to see if my money belonged to them.

When I asked my banker, flecks of foam appeared at the corner of his mouth and his eyes narrowed into glittering evil slits. He said I was either trying to unload some funny money on him, or I had turned into some Commie-pinko fascist piglet because it was completely un-American to even think of giving money away—in the unlikely event that I actually had some. Then he went off to check the balance in my account. When he returned he was a changed man.

"Perhaps you should seek help," he said, trying to suppress his laughter. "I hear they can do wonders for your condition with medication. Maybe you could take your $63.87 and buy two whole prescriptions," he concluded, collapsing on the floor in a fit of guffawing.

I am not improved as a human being when people are rude to me.

Meanwhile, the recession is worsening. Plants are closing, corporations are cutting back, people are losing jobs everyday and the yuppies are down to their last free VCR cleaning.

It suddenly occurred to me that since no one has money to spend right now except the government, which is doing so with its usual wild abandonment, my money should be returned to Washington.

So I called the CIA in Langley, Va., and asked them to tell me who in Washington is in charge of Wild and Abandoned Spending. I was immediately transferred to the Defense Department at The Pentagon, but the person in charge of spending couldn't come to the phone because he was out shopping for new and improved implements of destruction. "Why is he out shopping?" I asked. "Aren't we supposed to be cutting back on military spending?"

"Well, we are," the secretary said. "But Russia was having a buy-one-get-one-free sale on rockets and the accompanying red glare, and General Disjoint just couldn't resist." But she would be happy to transfer me to the person in charge of Wild and Abandoned Spending at the General Services Administration office.

"And would these be the people who spend six or seven hundred dollars apiece for new toilet seats?" I asked. "Oh yes," she said. "When it comes to spending money like there's no tomorrow, these people made the Defense Department look like a bunch of Smurfs. "And, she added, "thank you very much, but we don't deserve your money, and besides, we have all we need."

I was sorely disappointed to find that the person in charge of Wild and Abandoned Spending at the GSA was not available to speak to me because he was out shopping for new and improved porcelain facilities.

"But why are these people out spending money?" I asked the secretary. "I thought we were supposed to be cutting back on government spending. We're in a recession—aren't we supposed to trim the fat, tighten our belts, learn to live lean, etcetera, etcetera?"

"Yes, we are," she said. "But a big bathroom-fixtures company is having a buy-a-commode-get-a-fuzzy-seat-cover-free sale, and the office manager just couldn't resist. And, listen," she said, "thanks so much, but you keep your money; we've got more than we know what to do with. But call up the President's secretary, I'm sure she can help."

The President's secretary was busy typing up an invoice for the national debt, but, boy, was she glad to hear from me. "President Bush has just about used up all his frequent flyer points," she said. "But I think I can get him another round-the-world first class ticket if I subtract your $63.87 from the cost of one gallon of Air Force One fuel, carry the budget deficit and factor out the burden of unemployment until November."

Where's My Money?

I couldn't put it off any longer. I had to talk to my friend David, the psychiatrist. And that meant I had to get past his receptionist, Miss Merriweather—a one-woman screening device so effective that she stands in at the airport when the X-ray machines break down.

Miss Merriweather's rules for allowing me to talk to David are simple—I must answer yes to at least three of the following four questions:

Are you on the brink of despair? I'm actually past the brink, Miss Merriweather; I'm in the abyss of despair.

Is the bank piling your possessions on the curb and driving your car away? Yes, yes.

Do you suffer from non-referential anxiety bordering on irreversible clinical depression? Yes, but my anxiety is highly specific. I'm certain Jim McKay will cover the Winter Olympics in 1992.

Do you imagine that the inside of your walls are teeming with carpenter ants beavering away with tiny chainsaws and little hammers? Yes, but it's not my imagination. The blinking of hundreds of tiny neon signs flashing "Carpenter Ant Motel, Carpenter Ant Motel" gives them away.

Enormously pleased that I'm having a crisis of Jimmy Swaggart proportions, Miss Merriweather put David on the phone.

"Why do you always identify me as 'my friend David, the psychiatrist'?" he said. "I do have a last name, you know."

"Whatever happened to hello, how are you?" I asked. "I don't use your last name because I thought it would ruin your otherwise lucrative practice if your patients identified you with me."

"That's the most sensible thing you've ever said to me," he said. "Well—now that you've convinced Miss Merriweather that you're having a major go-to-pieces, what is it? Is it Derby again?"

"Oh, no," I said. "I've got Derby taken care of. First I cut the grass, then I leave town. It's not about Derby; it's about money. I…"

After David regained control of himself, he said, "What about money? You never worried about it before, which, I suppose, is why you don't have any."

"Well, that's the point. After the bottom fell out of the stock market, when everyone said they'd lost all their money, I thought I'd better go to the bank to see if mine was still there. They wouldn't let me see it, so I assumed they've lost my money as well. And not only that; my self-esteem declined 10 points when the teller collapsed from laughing at me like you just did. When she finally recovered, she threw some change on the counter and asked me if it looked familiar. I suspected she was making fun of me, so I said no, it didn't look familiar.

"When I last saw my money, it was green, not silver, and it had pictures of George Washington on it. At least the branch manager was nice enough to escort me out to my car after they called EMS for the teller. When I left, she was face down in the cash drawer, babbling about wanting to be a teacher while the governor seems to have lost the money for education. At any rate, he says he can't find it anymore and…"

"Wait a minute," David said. "Are you telling me you think you should be able to waltz in the bank anytime you feel like it and expect to see your money?"

"Why not?" I asked. "I can look at anything else that's mine anytime I want. Why can't I see my money when I want to? It's like visitation rights. Why can't I take it out on the weekends and over Christmas? Maybe a couple of weeks in the summer, or at the very least, spring break. David, are you all right? It sounds like you're crying."

"Me? No, I'm fine," he said, sniffing. "I'm just disappointed because I thought we got the money crisis cleared up in '82 when you went through Fear of Money Machines."

"Look, David. Life is hard. It took me all of the 70's just to figure out how to operate a three-way lamp. Then the 80's come out of nowhere with compact discs, VCRs, home computers capable of publishing an entire set of encyclopedias, answering machines that are so intimidating I haven't talked to some of my friends since 1979, television evangelists who publicly act out the Book of Genesis and floating discos that look like giant melted strawberry ice cream cones. Not to mention the three-point shot and the fact that Oprah Winfrey really believes she's an interesting person. God only knows what the 90's will bring."

"Wait. I get it," David said. "You need some reassurance that there are still some simple things in life, like the bank knowing exactly where your money is. Since nothing could be more simple than your bank account, I'll call the bank tomorrow and tell them it's critical to your mental health that you see your money. And I'll alert the SEC that the global monetary system may collapse temporarily while your money is out of circulation. Now, as long as we're on the subject of money, can I expect you to do anything about your consultation fees?"

"Don't worry," I said. "The roll of quarters is in the mail."

Smiling Through The Apocalypse

I was watching the evening news the other night when the anchorman, who was wrestling with his coat, reported that some experts believe we're in for a recession. At first I thought he was unnerved by this downturn in the economy, but I realized he'd probably just seen *Broadcast News* and was trying unsuccessfully to follow the movie's tip on coattail-sitting for a better on-camera presence.

Anyway, the news of the impending recession reminded me of a comment attributed to Betsy Bloomingdale during the energy crisis in the 70's. She was quoted as saying she would do her part to conserve energy by not allowing the servants to use the microwave after 6 p.m. I was impressed. What more could a rich person with a social conscience do than have her sitdown dinner parties for 300 at 5:30 in the afternoon when the rest of the working world is right in the middle of Miller Time?

I was relieved when the network took a commercial break because Dan was still thrashing around trying to get his coat under control. I took advantage of the time by trying to get Betsy on the phone so I could find out what inspiring sacrifices she plans to make when things get really tough.

Unfortunately, Betsy was busy supervising the clean-up crew from another early dinner party (those energy-conscious habits are hard to break) and couldn't be disturbed.

"Are you one of the servants who can't use the microwave after six o'clock?" I asked the man who answered the phone.

"No, I'm not a servant," he huffed. "I'm just here to look at the 32-cup cappuccino machine, the gelato maker, the six-oven restaurant range and the black French Aerospatiale Super Puma military jet helicopter."

I was pondering this interesting development when the evening news returned. Dan's eyes were bulging a little more than usual, but he had obviously overpowered his coat, which was now resting submissively on his shoulders. Relieved that Dan's media crisis was over, I asked the man on the phone why he was checking out Betsy's wares.

He said he had been thumbing through the designer edition of *Bargain Mart* and came across her For Sale ad, right next to John Connally's ad for a Chevy Suburban outfitted with a walk-in closet and a redeye gravy machine.

"I know John Connally is bankrupt, and he'll probably have to sell everything but his daytime Rolex, but why is Betsy advertising in *Bargain Mart?*" I asked. "Is she trying to get some cash on hand in case we have a recession, as reported tonight by an anchorman making a desperate attempt to improve his on-camera presence?"

"What? A recession? You must be a poor person, or at the very least a Democrat," he said. "Rich people don't have recessions. They might have the occasional reverse in fortunes, but it's only a temporary setback—not a recession."

"Oh, I see," I said. "So the rich person sells her helicopter and her kitchen toys as a hedge against a possible reverse in fortunes while the poor people and the Democrats have a recession?"

"Not in this case," the man said. "Rich people are selling their stuff because they're suffering status burn-out. The pursuit of material goods in the 80's exhausted everybody, but the rich people were already hard-pressed to stay ahead of the yuppies. It's no fun having everything you want if everyone else has it too."

"Does this mean people are beginning to understand that the frantic accumulation of material possessions is superficial and meaningless?" I asked. "Will there be a return to the real values of family, friendship, motherhood and green stamps? Will people eat real tomatoes and real Velveeta and drink real beer again instead of having wine coolers with sun-dried tomatoes and buffalo mozzarella? Can we..."

"Get a grip on yourself," he interrupted. "You're getting carried away. It just means the rich people are trading their status symbols for negative chic. You know—things like Disney World tote bags, real Melmac, K-mart sneakers, paper plates and..."

"Yes, I know," I said. "All the things the poor people and the Democrats have."

You Can Run, But Not Hide

had planned to run for president this year, but I'm having second thoughts after a reporter, disguised as a piece of lint, saw me kiss my best friend's husband under the Christmas mistletoe. Convinced that I was lacking the good judgment and strong moral fiber required to lead the country, the reporter launched a full-scale background investigation and found that occasionally I take more than the recommended two aspirin per four-hour period.

My political advisers, Sleepy and Goofy, believe that my mistletoe misdemeanor and my failure to read and follow instructions clearly printed on the side of the aspirin bottle will subject me to public crucifixion and humiliation.

However, like most political candidates who have disguised themselves as having nothing left to hide—I may reconsider and get into the race. With the results of my investigation now public, I'm sure there's nothing to lose; every detail of my life, both private and professional, is already a matter of public record.

But I don't blame the press for this lack of privacy. In fact, the loss of privacy has little to do with the press. My life is an open book because of these six insidious words: "Just fill out this application, please."

Following this directive over a period of years means that everyone from the paperboy to the gas station attendant knows my name, address, phone number, social security number and place of employment. Doctors and dentists, of course, know all that plus my date and place of birth, medical history, personal history, socio-economic background, annual income and the answer to that all-important question: Who's responsible for my bills?

The hospital has all of this information, plus it knows my religious preferences, whether I rent or own my own home, how long I've lived at the same address, my choice of beverage for evening meals, how long I've had a job and the whereabouts of my ex-husband.

The car dealer collects all of this information as well, despite the fact that he's only interested in who's going to finance my car; and the vet has the same amount of data, although he's most interested in knowing if my cat, Badman Trouble, has a trust fund.

My bank knows everything about me, including the whereabouts of my ex-husband (thankfully they keep this information to themselves) and the fact that my cat does not have a trust fund; otherwise it would have financed my car. The bank also knows how many credit cards I have and what I owe on them. And it knows that I don't yet own my own home, or much of anything else for that matter, except a dog whose only financial contribution is that he eats enough to qualify for huge refunds from the Purina Kennel Club.

My bank knows I've never filed for bankruptcy, how many times I've wanted to commit a felony and how many times I've borrowed money for home improvements. The bank is also pretty sure I used the money to pay the doctor, the dentist, the hospital, the car dealer and the vet.

The amount of information I've supplied on application forms would make Bob Woodward jealous. What, I ask, entitles total strangers with no more credentials than a printed form to be able to extract every detail of my life when the only information they really want is this: DO YOU HAVE ENOUGH MONEY TO PAY THIS BILL, AND IF YOU DON'T, WHO DOES?

I'm tired of giving away my life history just because someone happens to have a form printed up for just that purpose. Now I give away information strictly on a need-to-know basis. I'm very quick to point out that I AM RESPONSIBLE FOR MY BILLS. I add that that doesn't necessarily mean I can pay them, but they can certainly rest assured that I'm responsible for them.

My future as a political candidate may look dim, now that it's public knowledge that my mother is right when she says to me, "Nobody's perfect, especially not you," but I'm still considering the race; I figure my chances are probably better than George Bush's.

And for those of you who think Mario Cuomo didn't run for president because he's got something to hide, all you have to do to find out is read his check-cashing card application at the grocery store.

Of Mice And Men

My attention has been focused on the presidential race for months now, and when I consider all the candidates, both those who started and those who remain, I can't help but think of an Aesop quotation: "A huge gap appeared in the side of the mountain. At last a tiny mouse came forth."

In this case, several tiny mice appeared—a veritable trapful—and it leaves me weary to think this is all this vast country has to offer. I couldn't help but notice, however, that none of the tiny mice are wearing high heels or lipstick—at least none that was deliberately applied.

I'm always frustrated that there are so few women running for political office, and I'm especially frustrated now that there are no women running for president.

I think the country could use some nurturing right now.

I suspect the lack of female candidates has something to do with the fact that women simply don't have the proper credentials to be president. While women are just as good at name-calling as men are, most women prefer to sling mud behind closed doors rather than on network

TV, and while most women play bigger than they are, they just can't seem to get the hang of those darned sports metaphors. Most women would never get the sneer thing quite right while commanding America to "Read my lips," and, sadly enough, most women have a genetic aversion to over-the-calf socks and sensible shoes.

And, of course, women are just not good at womanizing. All denials to the contrary, womanizing is very popular with the voters, and those candidates who don't or can't, engage in at least a little womanizing here and there are at a serious disadvantage.

Women are also reluctant to run for president because so few women have a combat record to talk about like former candidate Nebraska Gov. Bob Kerrey, and even fewer women have an opportunity to make up excuses about draft dodging.

Women don't want to run for president against Bill Clinton because he's better-looking, Paul Tsongas is more earnest, and Jerry Brown is more sensitive. Little does it matter that Bill Clinton and Ivana Trump look so much alike they could have been separated at birth, and Paul Tsongas sounds a lot like Elmer Fudd. While a lot of people said "I like Jerry Brown," few would actually vote for him except for Eight Llamas In Search of a Public Facility.

How many female candidates could compete with Iowa Sen. Tom Harkin's early withdrawal? And is there a woman alive who could play as hard-to-get as New York Gov. Mario Cuomo? And what woman could do the job that Pat Buchanan or David Duke does?

On paper, there are women who have the same credentials as Bill Clinton. There are three women governors (Joan Finney of Kansas, Barbara Roberts of Oregon and Ann Richards of Texas), and 21 women in Congress. You'd think at least one of these women would want to run for president, but perhaps none of them has charisma.

Charisma, as we all know, is just as important as having an economic plan, a health-care plan, an environmental plan, and a frequent flyer plan. Paul Tsongas, as if he didn't have enough to worry about (what president ever had a silent letter in his name?) was so concerned about his lack of charisma that he declared his wife had enough for both of them, and Jerry Brown was so worried about charisma that he attacked Hillary Clinton. But she was busy not baking cookies and having teas and didn't pay much attention. And Texas Gov. Ann Richards was too busy being smart and funny to worry about being charismatic.

Women hesitate to run for president because they dread the inevitable public scrutiny, the loss of privacy and the constant criticism. They're certain that once they got in the White House and added more closet space, they would be criticized for cleaning house. And not only that, they would probably want to balance the checkbook and see that America got three balanced meals a day.

And then there's the inevitable criticism that women are too emotional, that power corrupts, but PMS corrupts absolutely. Which brings us to everyone's favorite subject—war. What woman has the stomach or the proper credentials to declare "This will not stand," and then engage the country in a swift and decisive military action that fails to capture the villain?

Confederate Gen. Nathan Bedford Forrest also thought

he knew how to win a war—"Get there first with the most men," he said.

Well, jeez. Elizabeth Taylor can do that.

Life Is A Carnival

When I was a kid I always looked forward to the county fair. I loved the horse shows and the sleek, fat calves with the rubbery pink lips and the cages of fancy rabbits. I liked the sparkling jars of crisp, green pickles, the cakes and pies and cookies and all the fancy needlework. To me, it all seemed "Best of Show" and everything deserved a blue ribbon.

But what I loved most was the carnival. I loved the booming calliope, the shrieks, the beautiful, mythical Merry-Go-Round animals, the sheer boisterousness of it all. I was fascinated by the people who ran the carnival. Young or old, they were gritty, world-weary cynics, unfailingly rude and unapologetically seamy.

I loved the spinning, whirling, jerking, spit-up-your-cotton candy rides, the games that never gave up the mammoth stuffed animals hanging all over the tent, and the urgency of the barkers pacing with their megaphones in front of the sideshows: STEP RIGHT UP LADIES AND GENTLEMEN, GET YOUR TICKETS NOW, THE SHOW'S ABOUT TO START AND WE'RE

ABOUT SOLD OUT. SEE THE SMALLEST MAN IN THE WORLD, SEE THE MAN WHO GROWS WATERMELONS FROM HIS CHEST, SEE THE FAT LADY COVERED HEAD TO TOE WITH TATTOOS, SEE THE GEEK BITE THE HEADS OFF LIVE CHICKENS.

When you're nine years old, what could be more compelling than the opportunity to see someone bite the heads off live chickens? I was accustomed to seeing my grandmother at the chopping block with the poor unfortunates destined to be dinner, but who could bite their heads off? Yuk.

I wasn't sure what tattoos were, but obviously they were naughty and should have my full attention. And a man who grew watermelons from his chest? It must be heaven.

The problem, of course, was finding an adult to take me in. Obviously, my parents were out of the question, and my sister's boyfriend flatly refused, correctly envisioning a sideshow of his own: SEE THE WORLD'S ANGRIEST FATHER PUNISH BOYFRIEND FOR TAKING INNOCENT CHILD TO SEE REALLY CREEPY SIDESHOW.

As it turned out, I had to wait until I was 14 and had a boyfriend of my own before I got to see the magic wonders of the sideshow. I was deeply disappointed that the man who grew watermelons from his chest was no longer among the cast, leaving me to wonder if the rigors of his profession had finally gotten the best of him, or perhaps it was just a poor crop year.

Other lesser attractions failed to live up to their billing—the half man/half animal was an old man with sad eyes and out-of-control testosterone, and the scariest thing about the snake handler was that the snakes he handled lived in a wilted cardboard box that threatened to come apart at every slither.

But I was enormously pleased with the tattooed fat lady who still remains the best demonstration of poetry in motion I've ever seen. She was an undulating 300 pounds of animated comic book action, a living billboard, the original performance artist.

I still regret having seen the man who bit the heads off live chickens. I tried to avoid it by looking elsewhere, but attraction to the macabre is strong, and I watched in spite of myself. It made me sick and it made me cry. Sick was easy to understand, but I didn't expect the tears.

I've often wondered since about the people who made up the sideshow attractions. At the time it made me sad because I thought I was face to face with a total loss of human dignity. Maybe so, but maybe there lurked among them a cosmic jokester, or those who seized an enterprising bridge between survival and homelessness.

But carnival sideshows are no longer part of the wholesome family image that county and state fairs now project. I realized that recently when I went to a county fair one night with friends. We saw perfectly-groomed riders warming up the beautiful gaited horses before the horse show, and we saw the perfectly-groomed fat calves and pigs, and rows and rows of fancy rabbits, extremely fancy rabbits and designer rabbits.

We rode the spinning, whirling, jerking spit-up-your-cotton-candy rides, but the people who took our tickets, fastened us in our seats and gravely offered their best wishes were well-scrubbed teenagers, unfailingly polite and dressed by L. L. Bean.

The only people who barked at us wanted to guess our weight, and there wasn't a tattooed fat lady or a live chicken anywhere in sight.

It was seamless.

Don't Break This Chain

Most things in life never cease to amaze me, but one of the things that amaze me most is the individual's capacity for hope.

We continue to hope that the next person we love is the one we will be bonded to for life, that the administration we voted for will bring peace and prosperity, and that the market's newest cream, lotion, pomade or snake oil will erase our lines, give us glossy coats and make our noses moist.

However, too much hope can cause brain-stem death; take for example, Procter and Gamble's eternal quest for a symmetrical potato chip.

But the ultimate expression of undying hope is the chain letter.

The chain letter, like Elvis and the cockroach, refuses to die. Empires fall, revolutions and civilizations come and go like dust motes in a wind tunnel, but the chain letter lives on, endlessly fulfilling its circular mission of nagging guilt.

Like most reasonably intelligent people who are occupied with the business of life, love and the pursuit of additional closet space, I had not thought of chain letters for decades. Then, from out of nowhere, I got two in the same week.

The first came from my friend Charlie, who lives in Minneapolis. Did he call first and ask me if he could send me a chain letter? In your dreams. No one ever calls up first and says, "Is it okay if I send you a four-page letter full of nagging guilt and false promises of good luck, success, money, fame and additional closet space? This four page letter and the accompanying 26-page list of former recipients must then be copied and mailed out to six other people within four days or you will awaken on the fifth day amidst the rubble of your former house, which burned during the night, and you will be covered head to toe with weeping pustules, and your friends, family, pets and business colleagues will shun you forever, and then you will have convulsions every 10 minutes until you die."

"Well, gee, sure, Charlie. I'd love to have a letter like that. Send it along."

The day Charlie's chain letter arrived, I tossed it on the table with three weeks' accumulation of other compelling letters from people who require my efforts to help them save bunny embryos, people who wish to make my lawn greener than springtime, and people who want to improve my culinary lot in life with hot pizza delivered speedily to my door.

On the fourth day, I poked the chain letter with a pencil to see if it would emit venom or spray spider eggs. After it settled safely back on the stack, I picked it up and threw it in the trash can. The bad luck that was promised for not sending the letter came the next day.

I got the second chain letter.

This one, from a stranger who probably picked my name out of the phone book, proudly claimed to have annoyed people around the world at least a dozen times, and promised that those who kept the letter going had enjoyed all manner of good fortune, abundant closet space and proof positive that Elvis and all the cockroaches of the world would indeed live forever.

But an evil tone presented itself for those of us miscreants who failed to send his letter out to annoy yet another six people. We were promised swift and serious punishment, up to and including fatal accidents and the loss of great sums of money.

Threats of any kind do not improve me as a human being. I was compelled to respond:

Dear Mr. Vicious:

Since chain letters, at best, are an outgrowth of an impoverished imagination, I trust you will understand why I discarded that pathetic piece of threatening trash that invaded my home under your signature. You promised bad luck if the letter were not passed on, and I am here to deliver it. At this very moment my good friend and guardian, Badman Trouble, is about to pay you a visit. He will patiently explain to you the error of your ways.

Badman is a gentle person whose heart swells with love when people treat each other with the dignity and respect they deserve. Badman is not amused when people attempt to prey upon the weaknesses or superstitions of others. When Badman is not amused, he is your worst nightmare. Just think of yourself as a sin Badman looks forward to committing.

Have a nice day.

Nine To Five

I've always loved getting up early in the morning. I'm irresistibly drawn to the start of a new day, full of promise, unblemished by things not done, promises not kept, deadlines not met. I start my day full of hope and high expectations that I can do all the things on my list, keep all my promises, meet all my deadlines.

At 6 a.m. everything is possible. I've got a jump on the day, I think, running in the park while the dawn just begins to streak the sky. My big dog, Tori, never runs, but ambles nearby while I circle the track. His expectations are also high: Did last night's picnickers leave a chicken bone or a half-eaten ham sandwich that he can have for breakfast? And can he wolf it down before I stop him?

Back home forty-five minutes later, the day is still new. One newspaper waits on the steps, the other lies in the dewy calla lilies by the sidewalk; each paper plump with local and national news which will arm me for the day. I still have a chance: I can do what I will for this day, but first I need to know what others have done in the hours that I slept.

Coffee—the first cup of the day—never tastes as good

at any other hour of the day—it is rich, bittersweet, the color of melted caramel. The papers provide the promised global superstructure, and some reassurance: the world in which I live is still intact, though its seams are splitting here and there.

I still have a chance to do with this day what I will.

But in the shower, the day falls on me with the same force as the water: Finish one column, write a synopsis for a new radio show. Call my mother—she's dreading the upcoming laser surgery on her eye; call the repairman—the dryer convulsed violently yesterday and strangled itself with its fanbelt. And what about my friend Jo visiting from Germany? When will I have time to see her this week? How will I get the final proofing on my book finished in time to meet the printer's deadline?

Before I can stop it, tomorrow's day rushes in on me, and the next day, and the next:

Pay bills, take Tori to the vet for his rabies shot, get my teeth cleaned, get a house sitter for vacation (how will I ever get everything finished in time for vacation anyway?) Another column due, two speeches to make, another radio show. Get my camera fixed, get the oil changed, get a prescription refilled, do the laundry, pay bills again. I've got four proposals out—what if they're all accepted before I go on vacation? What if even one is accepted? How will I meet those deadlines? Is it safe for Mom to have any kind of surgery with a heart condition?

STOP! STOP! It's only 7:30 in the morning.

I can do with this day what I will.

Meet one deadline, call my mother. Let tomorrow take care of itself.

I leave the house, repeating the mantra—I can do with

this day what I will—trying to quiet the demons that will now ride my shoulder all day long.

But in the early morning rush hour, my mind continues to sort and sift through the day's priorities, rearranging the list through a super-charged kaleidoscope. I stop at a traffic light, and look at the car in front of me.

The woman driving the white BMW convertible with the top down is gorgeous. She's wearing a black and white polka-dot dress, and large round sunglasses with bright-white frames. Her long black hair is wild and tangled by the wind, but she makes no attempt to tame it. In her rearview mirror I can see that her lipstick was painstakingly applied, outlined with a lip brush, and filled in with vivid red. Her head and shoulders move rhythmically with the rock music emanating from her tape deck. Her vanity license plate proclaimed I B TAN-N.

I looked at the car next to me—a dark blue station wagon of indeterminate origin. The woman driving the car is pretty. Her hair is breathtakingly short and doesn't need the pat she gives it with one hand while she hastily applies lipstick with the other. She drops her lipstick in her purse and touches the cheek of the little girl beside her. The little girl is crying and waving her shoes in the air. A baby sleeps in the car seat behind her, next to an effusion of diaper bags, books, tiny clothes, baby bottles, toys and a briefcase.

The light turned green.

The woman in the convertible sped away, still bobbing and weaving, her beautifully manicured left hand waving in the wind. I followed in my four-wheel drive, wearing a T-shirt and shorts, sitting next to a passenger seat cluttered with reporter's notebooks, a tape recorder, tapes, books, articles ripped from newspapers, empty coffee cups and Styrofoam reminders of yesterday's fast food.

The woman in the station wagon gripped the wheel resolutely with both hands, glanced in the rearview mirror to check on her baby, and drove on.

We will do what we can with this day.

Let's Take A Survey

Every day when I read the paper or watch the evening news, I get the feeling that Americans love nothing more than making up opinions about everything from the color of government cheese to who they would vote for if the election were held right this minute.

And not only are people willing to offer up opinions, (as well as comprehensive demographic profiles), they freely give those opinions to anyone standing in a shopping mall with a clipboard in hand, or to any TV reporter who pokes a microphone in their face.

But I'm always intrigued by news headlines that promise the latest results of a new study, the most recent poll or an overnight survey. I can't wait to read the stories that accompany headlines like "Study Shows Average American Male Hitches Pants Up 13 Times A Day" or "Survey Indicates Decline In Family Values, Spelling and Visits to Snake Farms."

Three questions always come to mind when I read these stories: Who paid to get this information? How will it be used? And what self-respecting human being would willingly admit that he has lost interest in belts and snake farms?

The public's willingness to offer opinions is exceeded only by the ever-increasing list of arcane subjects handed over to polltakers and marketing research firms by clients who have a need to know and money to burn. Since every study has a client, whether it's the government or private enterprise, some one may actually use the data after it's tabulated and analyzed.

For example, take the alarming results that snake farm visits are suffering a decline, and imagine how this information might be used by the client, Robert Ann and Mae Dimple Stump, proprietors of COIL ON US, a snake farm in said decline:

"Bobby Ann, according to this here report, the average American male is too busy hitching up his pants to take his family to visit a snake farm. No wonder family values are declining, and the average school kid can't spell 'potato', much less 'copperhead'. What are you fixin' to do about it? COIL ON US is one mouse away from shedding its skin and goin' under."

"First of all, Mae Dimple, don't call me Bobby Ann," Robert Ann said. "And while it's true that first quarter profits were down 73% vs. the same period last year, we have to consider all the variables: the U. S. recession, which produced a weak dollar and thus softened the global economy; the cataclysmic increase in the federal deficit, the ever-increasing cost of health care, the ambivalence of global warming and global cooling, the personal pressures associated with job loss, a decline in social services and a lack of luster in government cheese— all of which appear to stem directly from the current administration's lack of commitment to a strong domestic agenda.

"Not to mention the fact that snake farms are closely associated with an anachronistic Southern Gothic culture that our primary target audience no longer views as relevant or life-enhancing."

"Like I said, Bobby Ann. COIL ON US is goin' out of business faster than you can say 'demographics'. Now what are you gonna do about it?"

"What I'm going to do about it," Robert Ann said, "is re-define the marketing mix. First, I've analyzed the product line, and I think we need a better balance of domestic and foreign offerings. We have too many garden snakes, too many black snakes and too many copperheads. We'll take a few down to sun themselves on I-65, and then we'll import some cobras, a fer-de-lance or two, and a dozen black mambas.

"Once we've got our product mix just right, we'll go straight into a captive environment mode. I think the 'natural habitat' approach was ahead of its time. Apparently snakes don't have the sense of responsibility that must accompany total freedom; allowing the snakes to go wherever they pleased did not amuse our clientele, nor our insurance company for that matter.

"Finally, I've been thinking about how to position the business for the future. Keeping in mind the need to disassociate ourselves with a decaying Southern Gothic culture, the need to quadruple profits with the lowest possible cash outlay, and the need to attract lawyers to the target group, I've decided to expand the business and change the name from COIL ON US to STUMP'S VOLVO AND REPTILE EMPORIUM."

The Politics Of Fashion

I hate to be the bearer of bad news, but here it is: if you look closely at the new fall fashions, you'll see a definite influence from the 70's. While that news may appear to have the same import as announcing the availability of mail-order omelets or a plastic pop-up coffin, don't be deceived. Fashion is nothing if not a reflection of the times in which we live.

This, of course, is the really bad news. Taste took a holiday in the 70's, both from a political and a fashion standpoint, and we're obviously now so politically and fashionably impoverished that we must re-visit Richard Nixon and the Me Generation for inspiration.

I can't think of anything in the 70's that I want to revive. Certainly not Spiro Agnew, Watergate, the national anguish and embarrassment of impeaching a president, Gerald Ford or his pardon, Vietnam, the energy crisis and Billie Jean King and Bobby Riggs. Certainly not wide sideburns, the lingering peace sign, disco glitter balls and hairspray fumes lethal enough to level an entire singles bar with one whiff.

And definitely not the two-inch platform shoes that just

showed up on the fall fashion runways. Twenty years ago these shoes threatened women with death or permanent injury, saved only by alarming messages sent to the brain: "Hello, this is your spinal cord speaking. In order for you not to fall on your face every two minutes, bend your upper body so that it is parallel with your feet. Hold your derriere still for balance, cross your arms behind your back and slide your feet on the floor. Yes, I know it looks like you're trying to ice skate in big rat traps, but whatever you do, don't look up, don't take any steps and don't get your bell-bottoms in an uproar."

Fashion, as an indicator of political and economic times, used to be simpler than it is now. Skirt hemlines would rise and fall with the stock market and the mood of the country. During the 30's, after the stock market collapsed on Black Friday, Oct. 28, 1929, hemlines dropped like a rock. With some time out for shorter skirts during the carefree wartime years, skirts stayed more or less long until the 60's when hemlines got as high as Timothy Leary.

It seems that a great many fashion designers inhaled during the 70's as well. After the 60's mini-skirts and granny dresses, one of the most unflattering garments ever to drape a female form—the midiskirt—made a brief appearance, only to be rejected as roundly as Clarence Thomas asking Mother Teresa for a date.

Shortly thereafter, women said to heck with the whole thing and wore pants for the next 15 years.

But now what subliminal messages are the fashion designers sending us when they parade models wearing Cruel Shoes with skirts of every length? Are we sinking deeper into economic disaster with political candidates who have no platforms of their own? Does every skirt length represent candidates who try to be all things to all people? Maybe we don't have a leg to stand on, but apparently it is a far better leg if it were teetering on $500 psychedelic snakeskin platform shoes.

Even though the platform shoe reminds me it was once said that Queen Elizabeth's shoes were designed by someone who had heard shoes described but hadn't actually seen shoes, I think the fashion industry may even be a little too subtle in its messages right now. If they really wanted to comment on the economic and political times with their designs, I have a few suggestions for them:

The Retro Republican Look features a complete line of Family Values fashions. Hemlines nearly reach the floor, and the body is draped and covered from head to toe in duncolored sackcloth. The chest is tightly bound, the hair is covered and the look is accessorized only by a large button proclaiming "I'm No Murphy Brown." This look can be worn well by anyone willing to assume the attitude of an injured martyr.

The Young Democrat Look is bold this season with body-hugging suits and dresses in all the "We Won The Primary" colors. Suits are carefully tailored to hide any paunch that may result from excessive junk food while on the campaign trail, and a special Congressional suit comes with an extra pair of deep pockets. The Young Democrat line looks especially good on anyone who is blonde, slightly pudgy and forty-something.

Elvis Is Dead And I Know Why

With The Support Of Strangers

know that my attention span is short sometimes, but I must have slipped into a catatonic state somewhere between the late 80's and 1992, when most of the population turned into addicts of one kind or another.

I can remember a time, not so long ago, when an addict was someone who was dependent on drugs or alcohol—addictive behavior involving a chemical component.

But now, addict is used freely, and often cheerfully, to describe anyone who eats, gambles, shops or watches TV too much. And there are sex addicts, jealousy addicts, crying addicts and control addicts.

Odd support groups abound: Messies Anonymous, Procrastinators Anonymous, Debtors Anonymous, Neurotics Anonymous, Emotions Anonymous, and Women Who Love Too Much.

US News and World Report calls it "addiction chic." I must have been absent the day it became hip to be hobbled, but I think the rallying cry of the 90's is, "You're nobody unless somebody helps you."

This smorgasbord of addictions has spawned thousands of support-group meetings, thousands of self-help books (many sold in bookstores dedicated strictly to the cause), audio and video self-help tapes, and in-patient therapy groups. Any day now I expect to see a proliferation of new bumper stickers that proclaim, "Too many addictions, too little time."

Our language expanded easily to incorporate the vocabulary of addiction, and now one can say with equal ease, "Spike is a Presbyterian," "Spike is a dentist," or "Spike is an addictive personality."

But 'co-dependent' is the descriptor that has become the Pavlovian bell-ringing buzzword of addiction jargon. Co-dependent was originally used to describe people who remain with, and worry too much about, destructive mates.

Co-dependent (and 'enabler') is now being used to loosely describe a wide range of compliant behavior, including the simple compromises in life like giving in to someone else's choice of a movie or a restaurant.

If we've become addicted to addictions, then there are clearly some gaps in the support-group list that need to be filled.

For example, I think we need support groups for people who can't say no to clogging, and support groups for victims of yuppie accidents—people who get their hair caught in the sunroof of their BMWs, or those whose compact-disc laser light accidentally shot a hole through their brain.

Support groups would be helpful for the hair impaired, for pet singles (single people who only get invited out by couples), and for people who get melancholy looking at Calvin Klein ads featuring men brooding in their underwear.

A group seriously in need of help is nice people who eat

bad things—pig's feet, brains, tripe, snails and tofu.

A Self-Pity support group would fill a gap, but it would probably fail ("You never come to the meetings, but we know you're too busy and you probably hate us all, anyway"); and a Handwringer's support group would serve a good purpose ("Last meeting tonight before the world comes to an end").

Many support-group leaders, when trying to solicit membership or increase attendance, will shout, "Don't Be Afraid. You Are Not Alone. There Are Others Like You!" Now there's an inducement that's guaranteed to jump-start me into psychosis.

But that's fine; I'm too busy to go to meetings anyway. I've got to finish my book—*I'm Okay, You're Co-Dependent.*

I'll Get Back To You

On March 10, 1876, when Alexander Graham Bell spoke the first words over the telephone—"Mr. Watson, come here, I want you"—I expect Mr. Watson was thrilled to be the recipient of the phone call that would forever alter the course of human events. I'm also certain that 10 minutes later someone else called him up and tried to sell him some aluminum siding.

I have the highest regard for Mr. Bell because I know he meant well when he invented the telephone. He was renowned for his work with deaf children, and much of that work contributed to the theory from which he derived the principle of the telephone and its vibrating membrane.

But Mr. Bell made it clear, in that first sentence, how he intended the telephone to be used: to deliver short, concise directives. He didn't call Mr. Watson up to chat, or to try to sell him something, or to ask him what he was watching on television or who he was going to vote for. He called him up to say get over here; I need you.

My mother knew exactly what he had in mind. When I was a kid, Mom would call me up at a friend's house and say, "If you're not home in five minutes, you'll be sorry." Leaving a trail of sneaker-rubber behind me, I would muse on the way home why mother never called me up to chat. And she didn't change as I grew up. When I was in college, she would call me up and say, "Stop writing checks on your father's account or you'll be sorry." When I was about to get married, Mom called me up to say, "If you marry that man, you'll be sorry."

Well, Mom is always right, and I'm always sorry. But she does call to chat now that I'm responsible for getting myself home, overdrawing my own bank account and living with the notion that, for me at least, the best husband is an ex-husband.

However, those formative years of telephone directives and pronouncements left me believing that phone calls should never last more than a minute and a half; they should never be placed when you think someone might be eating, working or sleeping; and they should only be used to transmit life-altering information, such as, "Hello, this is the Publishers Clearinghouse Sweepstakes. We are happy to inform you that you have just won $50 million, four vacation retreats in the countries of your choice and the right to occupy the next vacant seat on the Supreme Court. Have a nice day."

But the ability to dial a few numbers and invade people's privacy has so much appeal in the information age that endless so-called improvements have been made on the telephone. You can now aggravate your friends in your own home by putting them on hold to answer yet another call; and you can even call someone while they're on an airplane. Being completely out of reach was the only thing I ever liked about flying, and it's extremely difficult to get the flight attendant to say you're in a meeting or that you've left for the day.

Between men and women, the telephone has been used as an instrument of hope—"I'll call you"—and heartbreak, when the phone never rings. And in the business world, the telephone is the instrument of power-tag—secretaries performing no-net maneuvers to make sure the boss is the last one on the line, and deliberately returning calls when the caller is expected to be out.

The answering machine is, without doubt, the most offensive outgrowth of the telephone. On those few occasions when I feel I have life-altering information to pass along, my news cannot be delivered until I suffer through two minutes of pre-recorded bulletins, announcements, directions and cute impersonations. "Hello. This is Richard Nixon. Please wait 18 minutes for a space on a new tape, then leave your message after Checkers barks. I'll call you back unless you're trying to sell me aluminum siding, and I want you to know that neither Pat nor I are crooks. Have a nice day."

The only good reason I can think of to have an answering machine is so I wouldn't miss the only other telephone call that, like the sweepstakes, can change my life. "Hello. This is Arnold Schwarzenegger. Maria doesn't like the way I play touch football. Can I come over and watch *The Terminator* with you?"

The Life Of The Cocktail Party

Whoever said he liked cocktail parties because they absorbed all the people he didn't want to associate with anyway must have been to a few dozen in his lifetime.

Sad to say, unless you're in traction or jail, cocktail parties are almost unavoidable. Like Boy Scouts and cat burglars, you must *Be Prepared*.

Two of the most important things you should know about cocktail parties are (a) what they are, and (b) why you were invited.

Cocktail parties are collections of 50 strangers who have nothing in common and who will never see each other again. Yet these 50 strangers will wear their best clothes and try to make a Good Impression just in case (a) someone might offer them a better job, (b) someone might remember their name for five minutes or (c) they might get lucky.

Now, why you were invited. It is not because the hosts like you or think you are scintillating company. The hosts don't even know you, nor do they know any of the other 49 strangers who will grind cigarette ashes into their

Oriental carpets, steal their expensive art objects or make off with their small house animals.

You were invited because the hosts saw you at another party and recognized your innate ability to hold a glass in one hand, a cigarette and an ashtray in the other, while eating mushrooms stuffed with peas covered with a fine morel sauce from a small green paper cocktail plate.

This is known to drummers as independent simultaneous single-limb coordination. It is known to corporate executives and heads of state as multiple execution of simultaneous priorities. It is known to hosts as the only reason you were invited.

Can you expect witty conversation from these 49 strangers as they peruse the art objects and small house animals? No, you cannot. The guest list will not show an entertaining mix of Iron Horsemen, corporate presidents, a rabbi turned standup comic and lingerie models. The guest list will be composed of 46 lawyers, two doctors, a tree surgeon and you.

The only weapon you have to ward off brain death is being prepared to entertain yourself. I'd like to share with you a conversational guide guaranteed to change the tone and manner of mindless cocktail chatter.

Read this question: "And how do you know the hosts?"

Now select a favorite response:

"John and I did time together, but I'd appreciate it if you wouldn't mention that to anyone else. I don't think the Board of Regents knows about John's past."

"John and I are having an affair, and we thought this party would be a good cover. But I'd value your silence on the matter."

"I'm an undercover rent-a-cop, and John and Mary

hired me to keep an eye on the expensive art objects and small house animals. But I'd rather you didn't spread that around."

And here are a few selections for the standard "And what do you do?" question:

"I'm a well-dressed pickpocket who just happened to see 49 cars parked on the street in this affluent neighborhood. But I don't think the others would be interested in knowing that."

"I'm a parole officer who accompanied that guest over there. Yes, that one admiring the Faberge egg. Why yes, I believe that is a little teacup poodle in his coat pocket."

"I'm John and Mary's marriage counselor. This party was an experiment to see if they could share an experience without killing each other. But I don't think they'd want anyone else to know that."

"I'm a movie producer, I did *The Color Purple, Out of Africa, The Fly, The Thing* and *The Flything*. My next movie will be produced by a limited partnership and if you'd write me a check for $10,000...Say, I wonder how this expensive little teacup poodle got into my coat pocket?"

Going For The Gusto

My friend Martini and I were power-lunching recently at Check's, discussing who among our friends had been injured during the after-Christmas sales, when she suddenly pushed aside her plate and announced that she was in love.

"Oh, no," I groaned, "not again."

She glared at me with that special high-intensity beam of hatred that only good friends and married couples reserve for each other. "What do you mean," she snarled, "not again?"

"Well gee, Mart—I didn't mean to hurt your feelings. It's just that you fall in love about as often as most people fill up their gas tanks. Anyway, what I mean is, who is it this time?"

"He's the real thing," she said, taking a sip of her Coke. "I've caught the wave. I prefer Max over Edgar. He's the heartbeat of America; he goes for the gusto, he eats what the big boys eat..."

I interrupted her in mid-babble. "Martini, did it ever occur to you that you watch too much television? Do you remember when you gave up watching cartoons because you fell in love with a guy who reminded you of Colonel Foghorn T. Leghorn? Have you forgotten the third-district cop who wore a pink T-shirt under his uniform? And what about the guy who swore to you he knew where the beef was?"

"Oh, shut up," Martini said. "You're so cynical. You haven't a romantic bone in your body. Max is different because he really knows how to live. He says he lives every day as if it were his last."

"I see," I said, thinking that if Max were present I would try to arrange for this to be the last day of his life. "And what, exactly, does that mean? How does Max live every day as if it were his last?"

Martini looked confused. "Well, you know. He works hard. He runs five miles a day. He learns a new word every day from his vocabulary calendar. He keeps his Volvo tuned up. He eats a different vegetable every day. And," she finished triumphantly, "he never misses *Wheel of Fortune!*"

I tried hard to keep my voice down, but the other power-lunchers had long since gone beyond eavesdropping on the conversation; they had quietly edged their chairs in a circle around our table.

"Martini," I said, addressing the group at large. "Don't you ever get tired of people saying they live every day as if it were their last? Do you know anyone, any single human being, who actually does that?" The group thought this over for some time and then shouted in unison, "NO WE DON'T. NOT ONE SINGLE HUMAN BEING."

"Good. Thank you, group," I said. Martini was staring at the attractive formica on the table top. I said, "Shouldn't your last day on earth be like making love on a roller coaster—exciting, dangerous, breathtaking—something you've never done before? Does eating cauliflower instead of peas really qualify for living life to the fullest?"

"ABSOLUTELY NOT. PEAS AND CAULIFLOWER ARE BOR-RING." The group was really warming up to the subject.

"At ease, group," I said. "Martini, if Max really lived each day as if it were his last, wouldn't he try at least one death-defying act—like going to a Harley-Davidson rally with a little yellow sign in the back window of his car saying, "I Eat Bikers for Breakfast?"

"BOY, WE LIKE THAT," the group shouted. "BIKERS FOR BREAKFAST. THAT'S A GOOD ONE."

Martini's eyes filled with tears. "But what about *Wheel of Fortune* and running five miles a day? That's really living, isn't it?"

"OH, SURE," the group jeered. "THAT'S SO EXCITING WE CAN HARDLY STAND IT."

"Lighten up, group," I said. "There's no need for hostility." I was beginning to worry that this was the same crowd that goes to a double-bill of mud wrestling and cock fighting.

Martini wept openly now. "Why are you doing this to me? You've no right to judge Max. If he says he lives each day like his last, then it's no business of yours."

"You're right, Mart. It's no business of ours. But the truth is, most people live each day as if were their first, not their last."

The crowd turned on me. "THIS BETTER BE GOOD," it shouted.

"Well," I said, "most people go quietly about their lives,

filling in the outline of each day with familiar, comfortable things. They eat at the same time and place, take the same route to work, watch the same TV shows, take care of the same kids, come home to the same spouse. Most people spend their time avoiding excitement and trying to reduce risk and the number of choices they have to make."

"SO WHAT'S WRONG WITH THAT?" This crowd was not only bloodthirsty; it was fickle as well. Their sympathies had clearly shifted.

"Nothing's wrong with that," I said. "It's just that these are often the same people who say they live life to the fullest, push each day to the edge and approach every day as if it were their last."

"WHO CARES WHAT YOU THINK?" the group shouted at me. "YOUR BEST FRIEND IS NAMED AFTER A COCKTAIL."

A Slightly Revised Story Of Civilization

I read an article recently in which the author ventured to name the 10 most important events of the 20th century. He included man's first flight in a heavier-than-air machine, the Bolshevik Revolution, miscellaneous international wars and the first moon landing. FDR, Lindbergh and Hitler also made their way onto the list, as well as the bombing of Pearl Harbor.

I didn't agree with all of his choices, but then it's an exercise in futility to list only 10 major events to start with. How do you choose Lindbergh's trans-Atlantic flight over penicillin or birth control? Did the bombing of Pearl Harbor have more far-reaching effects that the development of the automobile or television or the computer?

But the more I tried to focus on the big picture, the more I thought of the unsung people and events that affect our daily lives. I couldn't remember the last time I saw a list that included poor Lajos Biro, the Hungarian who invented the ballpoint pen. And no one ever gives credit to Donald Bailey, the inventor of the portable military bridge. Granted, I don't often have occasion to use the portable military bridge in the course of my daily life, but I'm sure there are a lot of armies out there that would be up a creek without one.

The quality of my life has been significantly improved because someone saw the potential in panty hose, credit cards, spray paint, street-vended chocolate-chip cookies and stick-on tattoos.

I've never regarded the telephone as a particularly helpful invention, but call-forwarding is definitely a significant achievement. What could be more convenient than punching in a random number and sending all your calls to a stranger while you take a nap?

And what about the drive-through window? Life wouldn't be nearly as much fun if I couldn't speed around buildings in parking lots, throw money in a window and get hamburgers or dry cleaning or cold beer. When I run out of money, I can speed around another building and exchange a piece of paper for cash and a dog bone or two.

I like the drive-through concept so much that I've entertained the idea of moving to Houston, the drive-through capital of the world. In Houston, you can whip through a parking lot, throw some money in a window and get your choice of a major household appliance, a four-piece matching living-room suite or a haircut if you're driving a convertible.

Of course there are some people who misunderstand the drive-through concept. They put guns in the windows instead of money, thereby getting their goods or services for free.

Another everyday occurrence, similar to the holdup in that it improves the lives of some at the expense of others, is the practice of writing people and asking them to give you presents. This mercenary practice is cleverly disguised with a decorative pink or white card bearing the euphemistic invitation to come to a shower. This is done to confuse you and make you think this shower of gifts appears out of nowhere, like air pollution and management directives.

This soft-sell approach momentarily lulls you into forgetting that you have just received a card that, in effect, says, "I am getting married, or having a baby, or both, or I am getting divorced, remarried, having new babies, etc., and I want you to buy me presents, the more expensive the better. Whether you actually attend the wedding, or the reception, or the baby shower or whatever is totally irrelevant."

The person who first saw the potential in the shower idea was probably the same person who invented income tax. "Now here's an idea," he shouted, smacking himself in the forehead. "Let's punish the people who have the initiative to work for a living by making them give most of it to a government that employs people for the sole purpose of piddling away the money they've worked so hard to earn." Why can't the government just ask us to buy them presents once a year?

Finally, no list of significant events, either major or minor, would be complete without Will and Ariel Durant. They didn't just list the top 10 events of the 20th century; they wrote *The Story of Civilization*. There's a certain arrogance in undertaking such a task; it appeals to me, but I have a hard time understanding what really motivated them to do it.

Maybe there wasn't anything good on TV that night, or maybe they just didn't like *Mel Brooks' History of the World, Part I* as much as I did.

Just Blowing Smoke

My dad called up the other day to see what was going on. "What's going on?" he said. "Did you get your brakes fixed? How about the roof? Are you seeing anyone who doesn't have a prison record? Are you still smoking?" My dad is like that. He knows if he asks me enough questions, I'll get confused and tell him the truth.

"Uh, I haven't had time to get the brakes fixed, but I've slowed down a lot, and the roofer can't come until November because he wrecked his Mercedes, and I'm not seeing anyone who has a prison record. At least I don't think he does. He has a bunch of little numbers tattooed on his palm, but he told me it was his therapist's unlisted phone number."

My dad mulled this over for a minute while I drew hearts and daggers on the wall, and then he said, "I'll bet you're drawing hearts and daggers on the wall; you always do when you're trying to evade a question. Are you still smoking?"

"Mmmm, yes. Sometimes I think about quitting but then I run another mile and forget about it. I enjoy smoking but it is getting harder and harder to smoke anywhere except in my own house. Airplanes, restaurants, public buildings, hotels—even friends and families—now segregate or terminate smokers with extreme prejudice. Don't you find it odd that while nothing is more complicated than a human being, we're now divided up simply on the basis of who smokes and who doesn't?"

"No, it's not odd to anyone but you," he said. "Smokers offend, annoy and aggravate most non-smokers. Most non-smokers couldn't care less about your health, or the environment, or pollution, or whatever. They just don't want to breathe your smoke in their air."

"Their air? Who died and left all the air to them? I rode with a skinhead cabdriver in Chicago a few weeks ago who polluted my air for 20 minutes ranting about white supremacy. Why don't creeps like that have to wear a warning notice that says, "My political views pose a serious health hazard to all those who are not white and/or Anglo-Saxon? Why don't they have to sit in a special section in restaurants for bozos only? Why don't…"

"Oh, please," Dad said. "Why do you have to mount a major crusade over every issue? You went on your first hunger strike when you were four years old. Your mother and I would've been happy if you'd had temper tantrums like every other kid, but no, you had to organize a protest against summer Bible school on the grounds that it infringed on your personal freedom. How you've stayed out of jail is still a mystery to me."

"Well, okay, so I get carried away, but I think smokers have been singled out for extreme discrimination, and I resent it. If Northwest Airlines can force me to sit next to someone wearing musk oil for three hours, then the very least they could do is let me smoke so I could think about something other than the many ways in which I'd like to kill or maim that person.

"Instead of promoting itself as a no-smoking airline, Northwest could increase its revenues significantly if it declared itself to be a no-musk-oil airline. And how about chatty seatmates? I'd rather sit next to a quiet, chain-smoking axe-murderer than sit next to someone who pelts me with his every random thought over the course of a five-hour flight."

"I'd certainly love to continue this conversation," Dad said, "but I'm sure you're late for a pro-choice rally, and the grass has grown about two inches since I called you, so…"

"But Dad, the thing that really gets me is these women in the mink coats who fan the air around smokers and complain about the hazards of secondary smoke. Did they give those poor minks a chance to complain about the hazards of being someone's coat? I don't think people ought to be allowed to wear a fur coat unless they can prove it was a road kill."

"Now wait a minute," my dad said. "No one would doubt for a minute that you're an animal lover and a supporter of protected wildlife. But don't you think your point of view is a little inconsistent, considering that you think the only good snake is a pair of boots?"

"Well, you can't blame me for being inconsistent. I can't help it. As you well know, I'm a Gemini, born of a Gemini father no less, and sometimes it's more painful than a triple-gum bypass."

"Oh, it could be worse," my dad said cheerfully. "The day may come when your favorite restaurant has a sign in the window that reads, "We Don't Serve Smokers or Geminis.""

Star Light, Star Bright

I look forward to reading my horoscope every morning as I beaver through the newspaper. I slow down when I get to the comics so I can commit my daily thought-crimes: "Please let this be the day Garfield chokes to death on lasagna;" "Please let this be the day The Terminator blows Mary Worth away." By the time I've wished Mr. Wilson well in his attempts to deep-six Dennis Mitchell, I've expunged my hostilities and put myself in a receptive frame of mind for my daily horoscope.

But when my hostilities are gone, my defenses go down and I'm far too vulnerable to take anyone's advice. If I read, "Go forth, Gemini, full of resolve to do your best, and you will earn great heaps of money," then I go forth with resolve and a wheelbarrow.

So the next day, what I want is an apology: "Dear Gemini, I know you felt ridiculous yesterday trundling around with the wheelbarrow, and I'm sorry. But you always believe you can make miracles happen, and it's time you got a grip. P.S. Go look up 'metaphor'."

Of course there never is an apology, so the daily cycle starts all over again. But part of my confusion lies in the fact that I never know the sign of the astrologer whose advice I read. So I've decided that the zodiac should have 13 signs, not 12, and it is the lucky 13th sign, Neon, who should give advice to the rest of us.

People born under the Neon sign would make perfect astrologers because they would never deal in metaphors, parables, Zen puzzles or Chinese water torture. Since the Neon sign always goes for the obvious and flashes brilliant, uncomplicated messages like "EAT HERE RIGHT NOW," or "EXIT ON THIS RAMP AND YOU'RE DEAD MEAT," a daily horoscope written by a person born under the Neon sign would always be right to the point:

ARIES—GROW UP! When you come home and find your socks and underwear in the rosebushes, and your priceless first editions in a raging inferno on the front lawn, your wife is not "sending you a signal." She thinks you are pond scum and would rather die than ever look at your face again.

TAURUS—Okay, everyone knows Taurus the Bull is stubborn. But it was definitely NOT A GOOD IDEA to throw yourself on the floor and scream, "I WON'T, I WON'T!" when the chairman of the board asked you to take his favorite client to lunch.

GEMINI—Little do you know, dear Twins, that Geminis are the Neon Sign—flashing on and off, on and off. One minute it's dazzling mental gymnastics and the next minute it's, "Wait, let me give common sense and good judgment a holiday; I can do this without a net!" You people are just too weird for words.

CANCER—Rumors are flying behind your back about you and a love interest. You may think you're in a high cycle right now, but when your wife finds out, you're a heartbeat away from dog food.

LEO—Your husband, the Cancerian, is looking for love in all the wrong places. Here Spot, here Spot, time for dinner.

VIRGO—Be responsible. Do your duty. Balance your checkbook. Feel guilty if you fall in love. THERE, ARE YOU HAPPY NOW?

LIBRA—The odds of getting what you want are about the same as those of Donald Trump inheriting the earth. Your partner no longer wants to unravel the mysteries of love with you. You should not have told him that he was the next step in vacuum technology.

SCORPIO—If you stop thinking about sex all day, you will get the raise or promotion you deserve. If you don't stop thinking about sex all day, your eyes will cross and all of your hair will fall out.

SAGITTARIUS—Venus is about to enter your solar house of love and romance. Venus is not a housekeeper. You do not have to pay Venus. Play nice with your friends and they won't throw your coat through the sunroof again.

CAPRICORN—Yes, we all know Jesus was one. But that does not mean you're God's gift to women. In fact, most women would be delighted if you disappeared from the face of the earth.

AQUARIUS—Your patience has been tested long enough. It's time to sting your ex-wife. Cancel your homeowner's insurance and burn down the house and everything else she stripped away from you.

PISCES—Words flail you, and yet you dream on. Your moon may be in Scorpio, but your head is under the electric blanket. Crank it up to 10, little fish, and have a nice day.

Hairdressing Up The News

For a while it was fun watching the local paper watching the local TV stations watching each other as the TV viewers tried to figure out where to watch what they used to watch before what they watched got switched to different TV stations.

It was also fun for a while to watch the stations stick their chins out and declare that station A's ratings could beat station B's ratings any old day of the week, no matter what network they affiliated with.

So there.

But the most fun of all was witnessing the stations' surprise upon discovering that, yes, TV viewers can still read, and yes, they did indeed find *As the Stomach Churns* and they didn't care what channel it was on.

But all this network-switching and changing and posturing was a wasted effort. All any station had to do to improve its ratings was simply ask me and I would have given them a copy of *The McCafferty Guide to Higher TV Ratings—The Complete Handbook for Braindead Station Managers, Written in Simple Sentences (That's Right, Not a Compound or Complex Sentence in the Book).*

The premise in the ratings guide is this: Change alone is not progress. Change, in order to produce the desired results, must be dramatic and cataclysmic. Switching network affiliation may ultimately be cataclysmic for the station manager who did it, but, in truth, switching networks alone won't improve ratings because all networks provide the same shows—they just have different names.

Thus, the key to improving ratings is simple—change the programming. And the first program to change is the most sacred program of all—the local evening news.

Every station manager in the country assumes that every living human being wants to watch news, weather and sports from six to six-thirty in the evening. THIS ASSUMPTION IS FALSE.

Well, okay. We do need some news headlines at six because news can change the way we spend the remainder of the evening. "WORLD COMES TO AN END; FILM AT 11" might cause some viewers to switch to the Holywater Channel for a few hours instead of watching *This Was Your Life*.

And since weather can also affect our viewing habits ("WORST TORNADO IN HISTORY OF CIVILIZATION TO HIT TYLER PARK IN 15 SECONDS"), we need the weather headlines as well.

But news, weather and sports?

I'm sorry, but the sports report does not improve us as human beings; nor does the sports report change our viewing habits for the remainder of the evening. Unless, of course, you decide to commit suicide upon discovering that you bet the farm on a losing team.

So, you may ask—news, weather and what? Well, how

about news, weather and hairdressing? Just think of the live-action-remote possibilities:

"Okay, Felicia, let's go live now to Heather Featherbangs in the nation's capital for a late-breaking update at Rosie Jeeks' Hair Salon."

"Good evening, Gary. This is Heather Featherbangs live in Washington, where today we've witnessed some of the closest shaves ever seen here at Rosie Jeeks'. First Lady Barbara Bush and First Dog Millie are sitting here in First Chairs, getting what we're sure will soon become the hottest haircut in the country—Twin Peaks.

"Here's Dwayne, First Hairdresser, for an on-the-spot interview. Dwayne, would you tell our viewing audience what you had in mind with the new Twin Peaks Haircut?"

"Of course, darling. But first, sweetheart, dumpling, you need some help. Talk about Helmet Hair..."

"I'm sorry, but we've run out of time. Back to you, Gary."

"Thank you, Heather. And that's all the news at this hour. Thanks for watching Haircut at 11."

No Pain, No Pain

Every ten years or so I re-stack the magazines around the house when I'm under pressure to locate key pieces of furniture and/or major appliances. I was forced to do this recently when a friend of mine, who's been coming to my house for 12 years, demanded that I produce the alleged sofa in the living room. Not only did he want to see it, he said, he wanted to sit on it.

Fancy that.

So the next day while I was moping around looking for the sofa, I happened upon a 1978 issue of a popular woman's magazine (the one in a constant state of excitement with every other line in italics) featuring an article entitled "HOW TO HAVE A PERFECT BODY IN TEN MINUTES."

Okay, I thought, I guess I could spare ten minutes for a perfect body, but not a minute more. I wondered why I didn't feel a need for a perfect body in 1978, but then I've been really busy since 1977.

I flipped the magazine open to the article only to discover, to my horror, that the secret to the perfect body was ten minutes a day of exercise. Yes, exercise. Mindless repetitions of deep-knee bends, jumping jacks, leg lifts and a whole host of other painful and unattractive things your body would never do if left to its own devices.

I hasten to point out that I have nothing against exercise. I do it all day long, every day. Granted, what I consider exercise has nothing to do with aerobic activity, cross training, weight training, proper diet or a decent night's sleep.

Instead, after years of careful research, I have developed a highly scientific fitness formula called $M = E$, or movement is exercise. In other words, EVERY TIME ANYTHING MOVES IT COUNTS AS EXERCISE. You, too, could melt away those unsightly pounds and inches if you only started recording the calories burned every time you blink your eyes, yawn, turn the radio on, or raise the fork to your mouth.

That thin person inside you will virtually leap out if only you give yourself calorie-consuming credit every time you put your head down and fall asleep when a Richard Simmons commercial appears on TV. Just imagine the fat melting away every time you hop on the bathroom scales or roll over in bed. And if you're one of those horrid morning people who bound out of bed in the morning, well, you've just burned up the bucket of fried chicken you ate before you went to bed the night before.

I think it makes perfectly good sense to take credit for the exercise that occurs naturally on a day-to-day basis. All other exercise, like algebra and a normal relationship, is unnatural and certainly never occurs in my day-to-day life.

Take deep knee-bends, for example. I honestly can't remember a time in my life when, in the course of human events, I slapped my forehead and cried "WHAT THIS

SITUATION CALLS FOR IS DEEP KNEE BENDS!"

And the same is true of jumping jacks. When Lee Iacocca found out Chrysler's profits were down 81%, did he leap in the air and clap his hands over his head? Of course not. That would be totally inappropriate behavior in the face of such a desperate situation affecting the job security of thousands of people, the gross national product, the world economy and the balance of trade. Iacocca wrung his hands for a few seconds and then gave himself a multi-million dollar raise.

Iacocca also recognizes the value of exercise that occurs naturally. Unlike deep-knee bends or jumping jacks, handwringing is frequently called for in one's daily life, and most people are sadly unaware that a few minutes of handwringing three times a week will cancel out that assortment of doughnuts you ate on the way to aerobics class.

Once you learn to give yourself exercise credit for every move you make, it will only be a week or so before you can count yourself among the Truly Fit. Being Truly Fit simply means that you are within 65 pounds, plus or minus, of the norm on the Human Being Look-Alike Scale. Being Truly Fit also means you will be peaceful and serene, say about a 10 on the Don Knotts-No-Doze scale. And, of course, being Truly Fit means that you'll never again feel guilty when you drive past the gym now that you recognize driving as excellent upper-body exercise.

But you'll really be Truly Fit when you stop thinking about exercise altogether, since thinking only counts if it's accompanied by handwringing.

Small Talk, Small Change

I was never very good at small talk because it always makes me think words are coming out of my mouth in tiny letters. How can tiny words have any meaningful effect on the quality of one's life? Isn't small talk like small change and small potatoes—too trivial and too meaningless to bother with?

I always thought small talk was throwaway fragments of conversation designed to fit those awkward spaces between human beings; like the conversational equivalent of Cheese Whiz, it takes up space but has no form or substance.

I've had to change my attitude about small talk, however. I'm still not very good at it, but I have found— through trial and error—that it does serve a purpose other than to make me wish I were dead when someone corners me with the revelation that he has discovered the ultimate weapon against bagworms and moles.

In my book, whose working title is *At Last—The Meaning of Real Life*, I'll add this chapter: 'The Meaning of Small Talk and Why You Should Care.'

Small talk is virtually the only channel of communication that is non-threatening, both intellectually and emotionally. It puts no pressure on us, makes no demands. Small talk eases tension and facilitates social interaction.

But the real purpose of small talk is that it keeps us from killing each other even more often than we do. It saves our social standing and it keeps us out of jail. Because small talk keeps us from *saying what we really think*.

When my neighbor says, "Hi, how're you doing?" he wants me to say, "Fine, thanks, how're you?" Not "Fine, thanks. Hey, has your mother made bail yet?"

I stand a chance of keeping my bones in their original order if, at the bus stop, I say, "Isn't it aggravating that this bus is always late?" instead of saying, "My, aren't you the fat and ugly one? Would you mind moving away from me? I'm getting cold standing in your shade."

During these everyday encounters, small talk is part of the connective tissue that bonds us and makes simple transactions more pleasant. The poor soul standing in the sweatshop searching the rack for my dry cleaning couldn't care less that my favorite post-Socrates philosopher is Hunter Thompson, and he would certainly not like to hear my views on fund-raising for foreign policy. He is hopeful that I will simply pay my bill with a smile, not gag when he tells me to have a nice day, and come back sometime.

Respecting the value of social small talk can also keep us in circulation. I doubt that I would ever be invited back if I had told my dinner-party hostess what I really thought when she asked me if I had a chance to meet the Smirks: "Oh, yes, I did. And aren't they a memorable couple. He even bored himself to sleep right in the middle of his monologue on whether the dead are affected by the fortunes of the living, and she said she'd like to borrow your dress and use it as a roach repellent."

And we have occasional encounters with imposing strangers when it behooves us to try to make small talk as politely as we possibly can. I inherited a gene from my father that kicks in every time I get behind the wheel. This bad gene has not gone unnoticed by those tall strangers who wear mirrored sunglasses and heavy hip objects. The same ones who have flashing-blue-light roof ornaments.

One of these tall strangers spoke to me about this bad gene one day. "What's your hurry, lady?" he inquired. "Going to a fire?"

"No, sir," I said. "I'm on my way home from the Policeman's Ball, and I'm trying to get there before midnight so my car won't turn into a pumpkin."

Pain has blurred the memory of the exchange that followed, but the tall stranger's words went something like, "Let's see how funny you are when you write a check for $86."

Uprooting The Other Wall

I wouldn't drive a hundred miles to go to my class reunion, but I flew to Berlin during peak travel season to see Roger Waters do *The Wall*.

Like my dad says, go figure.

I can't always explain my actions, nor do I often feel compelled to, but my dad pressed me to explain, thinking as he does that I sometimes have only a casual relationship with common sense.

"You went to Berlin to see the wall?" he said. "If you wanted to see the wall you should have gone before last November. They tore the wall down. It's gone. It's history. It's a former wall, an ex-wall, a no-more wall. People danced in the streets and poured champagne all over each other. Haven't you ever heard of the six o'clock news? Or have you been in a coma the past few months?"

I tried my best to explain. "But *The Wall* is not the Berlin Wall, Dad, it's a rock opera. It was a rock album first produced in the late 70's by a group called Pink Floyd, and it's about alienation and decay, and the walls that we put up to separate us from humanity, and…"

"Rock opera, schmock opera," Dad said. "Don't you

have anything better to do with your money? You still haven't gotten your roof fixed, and your house is so full of books and papers that it could catch on fire anytime you strike a match, which is far too often if you ask me. You could have spent the same amount of money and added on to your kitchen, or gotten rid of it altogether since it's nothing but an appliance museum."

"But this was a once-in-a-lifetime event, Dad. It was incredible to be a part of 200,000 people who stood on no-man's-land between East and West Berlin to see this concert. And I got to see two dress rehearsals in addition to the real thing, and, (pausing for all the dramatic effect I could muster), I got to meet Roger Waters and Sinead O'Connor and Garth Hudson and Cyndi Lauper."

"I'm sure they're all very nice people," Dad said. "But they don't sound like Germans to me. As long as you were in Berlin, it seems like you could have spent some time doing something educational."

"I did. I saw interesting museums and historic land-marks, but the most enlightening thing was talking to people. It was an exciting time to be there, though a little sad in a way because everything is moving so fast. Western capitalism is moving quickly upon people who haven't had time to assimilate changes yet."

"But aren't they happy about everything that's happened?"

"Well, yes, they're happy about it. But it brings respon-sibilities that are unknown. Many people have had a lot of decisions made for them for a long time, and now they're on their own, and in many ways it has to be a little frightening. And some of the changes are not seen as all positive."

"Like what?" Dad asked.

"Like the majority of East German women work, and day care, which has always been a given, is not easily available in West Germany. In fact, I was told there are long waiting lists for kindergarten, and private child care is unaffordable."

"But the thing that amazes me most," I went on, "is to think that these two cultures could meld easily even under the best of circumstances. West Germans have more in common with the Austrians or the Swiss than they do their own countrymen. The Germans share the same basic language, but they don't have the same vocabulary."

"What do you mean?" Dad asked. "If they have the same language, then they must understand each other."

"Well, basically they do, but imagine living behind a wall so long that you have no words for freedom, or words to describe any liberal beliefs."

My father was silent for a long time.

"So now do you understand why I went, Dad?" I asked.

"I do understand," he said. "You wouldn't drive 100 miles to come home to your class reunion, but you flew all the way to Berlin to see a rock concert."

The Kindness Of Strangers

I took particular note one night when Garrison Keillor told his *Prairie Home Companion* radio audience that you only travel if you feel bad; if you had felt good, he said, you would have stayed home. That sentiment struck a responsive chord in me because I've often made the mistake of traveling because I felt bad—sometimes from overwork, sometimes from heartache, or sometimes because of a really scary haircut.

Travel for escape never solves anything for me. If it's work I need to escape from, then I work day and night to get as much done as possible before I leave. When I finally fall into my seat on the plane, I am wrung out from exhaustion, strung out from stress, high-wired on caffeine and hollow-eyed from sleep deprivation.

I AM HAVING SOME FUN NOW.

As the trip gets under way, my attitude and my state of near-delirium worsens as each ticket agent/flight attendant/pilot mechanically announces that the flight has been delayed/canceled/rescheduled due to weather/lack of equipment/the decline of Western Civilization as we know it. These announcements are always followed by the equally mechanical exhortation to "Have A Nice Day."

The raging psychotic who resides in my dark side, barely concealed beneath a fragile veneer of civility, bursts to scream "HAVE A NICE DAY YOURSELF, YOU VACUOUS POD, WHILE I STRANGLE YOU WITH MY SEAT BELT, STUFF THIS LITTLE VOMIT BAG DOWN YOUR THROAT AND SHOVE YOU OUT THE EMERGENCY EXIT. CAN'T YOU SEE I'M TRYING TO RELAX?"

After arriving at more than one destination in less than an ideal frame of mind for a carefree holiday, I've found that the most effective and least expensive cure for the stress of overwork is not to add the stress of travel at all. I can safely vent my hostilities and re-center my being in a peaceful wash of serenity by spending a quiet weekend at home watching *Commando, Raw Deal, Predator* and *Conan The Barbarian*.

I've also found that traveling to escape heartache is no more successful than traveling to escape work. A broken heart doesn't mend any faster in Vienna than it does in Tyler Park, although I must say the quality of the heart-mending chocolate is considerably greater, as are the opportunities for heart-mending with Arnold Schwarzenegger look-alikes.

At any rate, after much travel trial and error (which has at least produced several hundred thousand frequent flyer points), I've finally identified the one variable which guarantees that I will have a good trip, and, on many occasions, a great trip.

The variable is simply this: an overwhelming, undeniable urge to be among strangers. When that feeling overtakes me, I am powerless in its grip. All I can do is buy a ticket because the trip is imminent, it is inevitable, it cannot be denied. At its best, it happens suddenly, but whenever it does, I'm history. (I wonder if that's what happened to my marriage. I always thought it was golf.)

Anyway, I'm not exactly sure what causes it, but the desire to be among strangers comes from a different place—a simple, powerful need to be on a new canvas in a new place with people I've never seen before and won't likely see again. It is not borne of a negative need to escape; it is instead a positive force which fills me with the excitement and anticipation of going to something, as opposed to getting away from something.

Being among strangers is a wonderfully simple concept that works well for me and I resist the temptation to analyze it. But I do know that its success has everything to do with the fact that I start off with a completely different attitude. My motivating desire, to be among strangers, will be satisfied, thus the trip ceases to be one of problem-solving and I go with no expectations. Then I am blissfully free to enjoy myself at my leisure, pursuing whatever I feel like doing at whatever time I feel like doing it.

Even having my hair cut by a complete stranger.

Come Fly With Me

When people say they love to travel, I assume what they mean is they love being in other places. I love being in other places, too, but find that travel, as it pertains to getting from one place to another, basically sucks swamp water.

Car travel makes me sleepy, especially when I'm driving fast; buses never go anywhere I want to go; and trains—the one mode of transportation I truly love—are only available in countries I don't live in. Short of taking a cab, which can be prohibitively expensive when you leave the country, the only remaining option is air travel.

Air travel, in my humble opinion, has finally been reduced to its lowest common denominator. Yes, the big Silver Budgies still get you to your destination faster than anything else once you're off the ground, but getting expeditiously airborne happens about as often as a relationship founded on respect, devotion, great sex, and rock and roll.

Living in 'The City the Airlines Forgot' certainly doesn't help matters any. A few weeks ago it took me longer (eight and a half hours) to get from New York to

Louisville than it did to get from Vienna to New York (seven hours, 36 minutes). While I slipped into a catatonic state at LaGuardia Airport waiting for the plane that would take me to Pittsburgh and then finally to Louisville, I fantasized about the day when my molecules could be exploded to my destination through the 'Beam Me Up, Scotty' method.

Since that day doesn't appear to be around the corner, I've decided to seek financing for a brand-new air service called The Anywhere, Anytime Airline Company.

AAA's greatest competitive advantage will be scheduling. Unlike other commercial airlines, which charge prices you can't afford to fly to places you don't want to go at times that are inconvenient for you, AAA will have over one million flights per day per continent.

The Triple-A guarantee is built into its advertising campaign: "Just Show Up and We'll Take you Anywhere." You never have to make advance reservations; in fact, you will be penalized if you even attempt to make reservations. All you have to do is go to any airfield, stand in line on the tarmac, and the dispatcher will hail an Anytime plane for you. Give the dispatcher $100 in small bills (after all, it is a hazardous job) and board the plane. Hand the pilot your destination on a slip of paper and you're off—anywhere, anytime. Nothing could be easier.

Never again will you have to put off that vacation to New Albany or Cementville, or that business trip to Fairdale, just because you couldn't get a good flight. Never again will you have to waste precious hours getting overly tired and emotional in cheesy airport bars waiting for a connecting flight. All of AAA's flights are non-stop, and they're all first-class.

Each and every seat is a reclining leather Eames chair equipped with a Sunnex reading lamp, complimentary mini-bar, a goose-down comforter and Blaupunkt stereo headset with soothing surf white noise. Prescription sleeping potions are readily available from each flight's medical crew.

Never again will you have to poke cautiously at polyester and urethane substances that mysteriously appear on your tray masquerading as food. The beef other airlines serve was never alive, the turkey was raised on a replicant ranch, and the breakfast you ate was the third runner-up in the airline-food look-alike contest. Anytime Airlines only serves catered meals from the four-star restaurant of your choice.

Cheerful AAA flight attendants will stow all of your bags under their seats, rock your baby, read you to sleep, give you a back massage when you wake up and drive you to your destination upon arrival.

Just in case potential investors are still uncertain about the financial future of Anywhere, Anytime Airlines, I'm sure I can win them over when I tell them smokers are always welcome at AAA Airlines; all flights, regardless of duration, will be smoking flights. Smoking will also be permitted in the aisles and during take-off and landing. All passengers departing Standiford Field, however, will be instructed not to breathe when flying over the Hurstbourne Lane air-pollution zone.

Lost In Space

A man driving a late-model pimpmobile pulled up next to me at a traffic light recently and asked how to get to Montana. I told him to go straight for 23 hours and hang a right when he got to Wyoming. He waved appreciatively and sped away toward Rhode Island.

My dog Tori, occupying his usual two-thirds of the car, started to growl and dragged the *Intergalactic Directory for the Geographically Impaired* out of the glove box. Tori always growls when I speak authoritatively on subjects I know nothing about, or when I lie to him, as I always do when I have to leave town. ("Don't worry, I'll be right back," I invariably say, throwing two suitcases out the door to a waiting cab driver. "Take messages, cover up the pool table when you're finished, and no more 'poor me' calls to the Humane Society.")

Tori pawed through the book until he found the 'How to Direct Someone to Montana if You're at the Corner of Bardstown Road and Eastern Parkway' section and looked at me reproachfully. When we got home, two hours and two blocks later, I wiped the dog slobber off the book and checked the directions I'd given the man who was now flooring it toward Rhode Island.

The directory got right to the point: "If you were at the corner of Bardstown Road and Eastern Parkway and told someone he'd get to Montana if he drove straight for 23 hours and turned right in Wyoming, YOU ARE A MAP MORON, A GEOGRAPHY GEEK, AN ATLAS AIRHEAD, A TRAVEL TINYBRAIN AND A MIND-LESS MEANDERER. AND NOT ONLY THAT, YOU'VE SENT SOME POOR FOOL HALF WAY TO RHODE ISLAND BY NOW."

Having ridden in more than my share of New York taxis, I thought I was impervious to being flailed by the printed word (DON'T SMOKE, DON'T EAT, DON'T SPIT, DON'T SING, DON'T GIVE ME DIRECTIONS—I CAN'T SPEAK ANY LANGUAGE) but I was stung by the directory's arbitrary name-calling over what I thought were pretty straightforward directions.

The next paragraph in the guidebook suggested that I might have made a greater contribution to efficient world travel if I hadn't slept through my geography classes, and outlined a two year remedial program at night school.

Since I couldn't stay awake during day school, I figured my chances for staying awake during night school were pretty slim. I threw the directory away, deciding instead to share with you some secrets on 'How to Avoid Being Called Names When you Tell People Where To Go: Compensation Techniques for the Directionally Disabled.'

My favorite technique is 'INTIMIDATE THE DRIVER.' Keep in mind that this only works once on the same person, and it never works with a spouse. If you've been assigned navigational duties, snap the map open smartly, jab your finger at any spot on the map (it's likely to be somewhere near Greenland) and firmly announce, "Here we are!" Next, talk as fast as you can, rattling off street names: "Go down Fifth Street 14 blocks, turn right on Main, go three blocks, take the 1-71 exit east, get off at exit 34 and take Eastern Boulevard to the stockyards. The restaurant is right next door."

Fold the map and throw it back in the glove box. Then accuse the driver of making his first mistake: "Oh, I think you should have turned there. The bypass would have saved us 42 miles. Oh, never mind, the restaurant is probably not too crowded anyway."

Another good technique is called 'STUN THE STRANGER.' If an out-of-towner asks you for directions, by all means be obliging. At that moment you are the city's goodwill ambassador, demonstrating our characteristic blend of hospitality and the love of having fun at the expense of others.

For those few minutes while you're giving the stranger directions, he will experience a false sense of security, which, as anyone knows, is better than no sense of security. Be lavish with your directions; give colorful examples. Be sure to tell him the Watterson Expressway was built during Junior Achievement Week, and that he will have roughly two and a half seconds in which to enter the flow of traffic. Offer to repeat the directions if necessary, but do not write them down, and do not introduce yourself. After he drives into the Ohio River, he may be inclined to look you up again.

Finally, never offer directions to an airline pilot, and when you're reading a map, don't send the driver through the big blue spots.

Elvis Is Dead
And I Know Why

Elvis, like the parrot in my favorite Monty Python sketch, is dead. He has ceased to be; he's gone, passed on, finis. He is a formerly living person, an un-alive person; he is a hopelessly, irretrievably dead person.

I'm sorry, and so is Brenda Lee.

I've always been an Elvis fan, so I was delighted to hear the rumors that Elvis is alive. I always thought Elvis was still alive anyway, living somewhere in celebrity limbo with Jimmy Hoffa and John F. Kennedy.

I was still holding out hope when I recently visited Graceland. But after spending the morning touring his home, I can assure you that Elvis is dead, and it had nothing to do with drugs or fat or fast living or tripping on bell-bottomed trousers.

Elvis died of bad taste.

Oh, sure, you scoff. Lots of people outlive bad taste, and some of you right this minute are naming at least six of your friends, a couple of hotels and a large, lumpy river restaurant just to prove it.

Well, that's chicky-and-bunny stuff compared to

Graceland—the undisputed intergalactic captial of bad taste. Graceland, featured monthly in *Architectural Unrest,* is the home-interior equivalent of Robin Givens, Tammy Faye Bakker, Eddie Murphy and George Bush's choice for vice president.

Touring the house, I found it easy to picture how Graceland evolved, starting with conversations Elvis had with Nigel, his decorator.

Nigel, I imagine, offered up the following: "Elvis, I'd like to do the living room in off-white so the eye will not be jarred or confused. The color will provide a perfect background for the works of Frank Stella and Sam Francis, artists I'm sure you'll want to collect, and then we'll cover the walls in silk jute, and..."

"Jute, schmute," Elvis said. "Ah want a 21-piece sectional couch covered in blue suede, like mah shoes, and ah want mah gold-leaf piano, orange shag carpet and some red flocked wallpaper. And ah want a lot of pictures of those little chirren with the big eyes."

"Right," said Nigel, moving on to the dining room.

Elvis yawned. "Is this the room where we eat? Well, ah'd like a dinette table and eight chairs. Chrome and formica. And one of those swag lamps with those little pieces of colored glass in them. And you can balance that effect with a big arrangement of plastic flowers in the middle of the table."

"Right," said Nigel, making up a shopping list.

"And while you're at it, Nigel, get me one of those black-panther lights for the TV, a couple of dozen yellow rhinestone pillows for the blue couch, and a big ol' clam-shaped bed covered with acrylic fur."

"Right," said Nigel, racing for the door.

Later that day, when the Wal-Mart truck arrived with the furniture, Elvis summoned Priscilla to supervise the delivery. Priscilla ran sideways through the door so she wouldn't bump her laquered beehive hairdo.

"Oh Elvis, I'm so excited that the furniture is here. We'll build another wing for the hairspray cans, and we can put your teddy bears on the king-size clam-shell bed, and your black-velvet paintings in the bathroom. I'll put the purple neon Twinkie light over the front doorbell, and I'll get your mother's pink Cadillac out of the den, and…

"Elvis, honey, what's wrong? You're turning green. You really shouldn't breathe around my beehive. You know what those hairspray fumes do to you. Elvis, wake up! Speak to me! ELVIS, GET UP! ELVIS, OH, NO, NO, NO…"

Here's to you, Elvis, wherever you are.

Your panther light is still glowing, and I'm glad.

Say You're From Syracuse

Fortunately, one of my close friends is a psychiatrist. But his receptionist will only let me speak to him on the phone about once every four years—and then only if she thinks I'm having a major go-to-pieces in a foreign country.

"What's that noise? Where are you?" Miss Merriweather shouted at me over the phone the last time.

"It's gunfire. I'm in Iran," I shouted back as I crackled aluminum foil into the receiver from my kitchen in Tyler Park. "Could I please speak to David? I'm having a major go-to-pieces in a foreign country."

"I don't know," she said, stalling. "The last time you told me you were under siege in a shoe store in the Philippines with Imelda and then there was that lame story about wild sheep in the Falkland Islands..."

"I'm hit...get David on the phone, you witless slug." I choked through three coffee filters.

"Oh, okay," she grumped. "But you'd better come back from Iran in a pine box or I'll never let you speak to him again."

I was making a mental note to talk to David about Miss

Merriweather's twisted logic when I heard his voice on the phone. "So what is it this time?" he asked cheerfully. "Lose your skate key? Having a recurrent attack of Fear of Fruit? Bloomingdale's burn down?"

"Worse," I said gloomily . "It's Derby."

"So what's so bad about Derby?" he asked. "What've a few hundred thousand screaming strangers ever done to you?"

"Oh, nothing," I said. "Except I think a couple of thousand of them are coming to visit me."

"What do you mean, coming to visit?" he asked. "As in staying at your house, sleeping over, eating your food (perish the thought), being entertained by you, etcetera, etcetera?"

"I'm afraid so. It all started about a year ago. I was on the plane to Tulsa and Oral Roberts sat down next to me and asked me where I was from and I said Louisville and he said he'd always wanted to come to the Derby and that he'd be happy to name me president of his university and give me half of his phone-ins if he and his wife could be my houseguests for Derby so I said okay and it's actually been kind of nice to be a big university president and have two million dollars at my disposal.

"And then a month later I was on a plane to Dallas and Trammel Crow sat down next to me and asked me where I was from and I said Louisville and he said he'd always wanted to come to the Derby and he'd be happy to make me a partner in the largest real estate development company in the world if he and his family could be my houseguests for Derby and I said okay.

"And I can't complain because T. Boone Pickens started calling every night wanting to buy me out and I always said no until he said he'd give me Shell, Exxon, ATT and four high-tech up-and-comers in the Silicon Valley if I would let him and his guests come to my house for Derby. He said he'd already bought the Seelbach, the Brown and the Hyatt but they wouldn't give him rooms because they'd been sold out for eleven years and so what could I do?

"And then Dennis Conner called and said I could have the America's Cup if he and his crew could come and I said oh okay what's a few dozen more at this point?"

There was a momentary pause in the rather rude snoring sounds on the other end of the line, and David said, "So what's the problem? You've met all these famous people and now you've got so much money you can even afford to pay me."

"I wouldn't go that far," I said. "Although it's true—I now own a dozen companies worth over a hundred billion dollars and Oral lets me do all the recruiting for his basketball team and the America's Cup makes a real attractive hood ornament. But how do I tell these people I sold my house to William Randolph Hearst?"

How To Dress
For The Derby

On the first Saturday in May, thousands of people will converge upon Churchill Downs in Louisville for the running of the Kentucky Derby. Most of them labor under the false impression that this world-famous event has some something to do with horse racing.

I'm sorry, but the Kentucky Derby has nothing to do with horse racing.

Well, okay, sure, there are horses there, and they do race, and people do bet on them, and the horse who wins the Kentucky Derby gets a lot of parting gifts, expensive network TV time, and a big kiss from our governor.

But the Kentucky Derby is really about the clothes you wear.

Yes, friends, if you've got a righteous wardrobe, you can forget the scratch sheets and the hot tip on Tripod in the third race; don't even worry about getting directions to the track once you get to Louisville. Just follow the migraine-inducing array of nuclear-neon hot pink, purple, and red and yellow silk dresses, the madras sport coats, the sunglasses and the pinwheel hats.

And that's just the Louisville Police Department.

Since the Kentucky Constitution guarantees the right of all Derby-goers to be entertained by what others are wearing, you must understand the guidelines for choosing the clothes you plan to wear to the Derby. And don't worry—if you lose your head and bring along something tasteful to wear, a member of the Derby Wardrobe Committee will be standing by to cheerfully assist you.

The first thing you should do is look for a store in your hometown that sells clothes loud enough to attract snakes, produce instant night blindness, and make Republicans weep. This store will not appear in the phone directory under any heading that includes the words "couture," "French," "designer," "elegant," or "understated." The store you're looking for is in a discount outlet mall two blocks from your neighborhood nuclear-power plant, and it will be between Hog's Tattoo and Snacks Emporium and The Rayon Teddie Palace.

The right store for your Derby wardrobe has a name like "Sandrella's House of Style," and since this is the most important fashion event of the spring season, go right to the top and ask for Sandrella herself. If Sandrella is well into a comfortable middle age and wearing at least two of her foundation garments on top of her stretch mini-dress, and if Sandrella's hair is sure to glow in the dark, you'll know you're in the right place. Just tell her you're headed for the Kentucky Derby and she'll know exactly what to show you.

If Sandrella does her job right, she'll impound your classic Chanel pearls and your Donna Karan navy blazer, but she'll let you keep your bodystocking on when you try that little string dress that comes attractively packaged in a souvenir demi-tasse cup. When you leave Sandrella's you should have all the basics for a perfect Derby outfit: a clear plastic bustier with tiny French angel fish swimming around in the cups, a Brain-Implosion Red satin micro-mini skirt, rhinestone-studded silver lurex stockings, and Terribly Turquoise suede sling-backs with five-inch heels.

But your Derby outfit is not complete without a hat. Buying a hat is easy when you know that your hat must be large enough to (a) create shade for a family of six, (b) block the view of at least ten people sitting behind you, or (c) be mistaken for an above-the-ground swimming pool. Once you've found the hat, take it home and decorate it with a couple of baby moon hubcaps, two silver Mint Julep cups, a half-dozen country ham-on-beaten biscuits, a disco glitter ball and a litter of St. Bernard puppies.

All you have to do now is see that your husband or boyfriend is suitably wardrobed and you're ready to roll. Getting the man in your life ready for the Derby is much easier; just let him take his normal golfing attire, add some white plastic shoes, a white belt and a pair of battery-operated socks in neon lime green that flash the message "We're Having Some Fun Now," and get him a new Panama hat; decorate it with a quart of Kentucky bourbon and a long sipping straw and you're in business.

When all your shopping's done, you'll know you have the perfect Derby wardrobe if you can answer yes to the following questions:

1. Would my Derby outfit frighten small children?

2. Has my kid ever thrown up anything that looks like this?

3. Does Kool-Aid come in this color?

4. In the event of a nuclear holocaust, could a rescue

team spot me from at least 100 miles away?

Now all you have to do is add that button that says "I'm An Out-of-Town Derby Guest and You're Not," and we'll see to it that you have a great time at the Derby.

We have to, because it's the law. Out-of-town guests must have a great time at the Derby; after all, it's guaranteed in the Kentucky Constitution.

The Couch Potato Rap

Trend-watchers say the latest thing in going out is staying home. "Couch potato" is a relatively new descriptor for the stay-at-homes whose principal pastime is watching television. One New York consulting firm, whose fees are roughly equivalent to Tammy Faye Bakker's mascara budget, more broadly defines this new stay-home trend as "nesting."

However the trend is defined, the trend-watchers agree that those who can most easily afford an expensive evening out are now staying home because virtually everything one needs for entertainment can be had at home. First there was cable television, which offers viewers a dizzying array of choices, ranging from docudramas such as *Baton Twirlers Get Sports Injuries, Too* to *Shelflife: The Movie.*

Now first-run movies are being rushed into video cassettes after only six months, which means the entire family can stay at home and enjoy the latest in violence and gore for only two bucks. Hot buttered popcorn is as close as the microwave, and you don't have to share the bathroom with strangers.

Even though these affluent stay-at-homes represent one of the newest trends, they run the risk of losing their place at the leading edge because they choose to keep up with only those trends they read about in the Sunday New York Times. Let's face it, some things just can't be brought into the home. Since I occasionally venture into the netherworld, it is my duty to report on two such trends so the stay-at-homes can continue to be in the vanguard.

One of the latest trends in club entertainment is 'male exotic dancing'. Simply stated, this means men come out and take their clothes off for women. When women do this for men, it is not called female exotic dancing, it is called stripping. The reasons for this distinction are worthy of discussion, but let's go on.

Attitude is the most important thing when approaching an evening with male exotic dancers. When your best friend calls to talk you into going with her, the following attitude is incorrect and will cause you to have a very bad time: "You want me to get dressed up (whine), drive 20 miles to a sleazy hotel lounge (whine), pay good money (moan), sit with two hundred screaming women (whine) and watch men dance while they're taking off funny costumes? HAH!"

The following attitude is correct and will cause you to have a very good time: "Wow! I could wear my new strapless knit mini-dress that almost got me arrested while I was still in the dressing room! And if we get there early, we could sit so close to the stage that we could see the oil on all those glistening bodies that are dancing just for our personal pleasure! ALL RIIIGHT!"

Once your attitude is properly adjusted, you can tell you're having fun because you're not looking around to see if someone's there who knows you. And you'll for sure be having fun when the cute blonde sheds his abbreviated Johnny Reb costume just for you. When you stuff a $5 bill into what's left of his breviates, that's when you know he's having fun.

Now let's examine another trend that the whole stay-at-home family should know about. The hottest thing in music today is rap. Unlike male exotic dancing, the beauty of rap is that you don't have to experience it firsthand to reach your full potential as a human being.

Here's how you can duplicate rap at home: Take the album your aunt gave you for Christmas, "A Night of Comedy With Richard Nixon," spin the turntable as fast as you can with one hand while scraping your $200 needle over it with the other hand. Breathe as hard as you can and shout rhymes made with four-letter words into Mr. Microphone.

Rhyming with four-letter words is not as hard as you think when you consider what you have just done to your expensive needle. When you run out of four-letter words, you can still rap with lyrics like this: "I'm too hip/I'm too cool/I'm too dumb for nursery school."

Even the best rappers run out of rhymes sometimes, so you can even get by with a lyric like this: "My dog Jake is one cool dude/my dog Jake shoplifts his food/my dog Jake is dead."

The only other thing the stay-at-homes need to know is that Michael Jackson is still trying to buy a dead person.

Ladies Lingerie,
Fourth Floor

My friend Marty likes to probe the depths of others' psyches by asking what they expect to see behind closed elevator doors. I think it's an interesting question that not only reveals the richness of our fantasies, it also offers a glimpse of the fears that lie on the periphery of our dark side.

One movie buff was quick to offer up a fantasy of the closed elevator as a relief for sexual tension, vividly recalling the frenzied elevator sex scene between Michael Douglas and Glenn Close in *Fatal Attraction*. A devoted fan of the hard-boiled detective novel and "Murder, She Wrote" said she always expects to see a dead body fall face forward when the elevator doors open. But one friend of mine said ruefully that closed elevator doors would always remind him of the day a smooth operator picked his pocket in a hotel elevator.

My own dark side fantasies about elevators spring directly from fear, but not fear of what I might see when the doors open if I'm waiting to get on one. What I dread, and what I try to avoid, is getting on an elevator alone at night. My heart is always in my throat when it stops at another floor because I'm sure Hannibal Lecter is standing there waiting to get on with me.

Despite my Bukowski-like fantasy called "Elevators Are Dogs From Hell," my expectations pretty much match reality when the elevator doors open during the workday: I'd expect to see a dozen or more briefcase sandwiches—men and women in suits pressed between their briefcases, staring straight ahead. They stand, hollow-eyed and stiff, with their arms tight against their bodies, trying not to touch each other.

Everyone acknowledges the unwritten rules of elevator behavior: No one talks, no one laughs, no one does the bunny hop.

But each one silently prays that the elevator moves swiftly to each appointed floor—"Please, God, don't let me get stuck between floors with these people. The woman standing next to me is one contraction away from having triplets, and the man standing in front of the doors has that desperate look about him that suggests his nerves are shot and his digestive tract is about to follow."

If I were waiting for an elevator at the end of a workday, I'd expect to see the same people, still protected from the press of other human flesh by hard-bodied briefcases, each individual sealed in an envelope of silence. They still stare straight ahead, hollow-eyed, doggedly observing the unwritten rules of elevator behavior: no one yodels, no one tap dances, no one asks "Do you come here often?"

But the jaws that were set in grim resolution at 8 a.m. are now slack; the squared shoulders now sag with fatigue. These people may be relieved to be leaving the workplace, but they are not happy.

These people are not happy because they must now

exchange one steel box for another. They must wander the multi-level concrete desert in search of their cars in order to face rush hour.

I've always thought the way people behave in elevators is a curious and interesting study of human social interaction. Elevators tend to make people subdued and courteous, two attributes not commonly found in other places where strangers are randomly thrown together. People try very hard to protect their personal space inside this tiny box, and they rarely talk except to make polite announcements and requests: "Excuse me, this is my floor," or, "Would you push five, please?"

And it's a good thing people keep quiet instead of saying what they really think: "ARE YOU PEOPLE CRAZY? WHAT WERE YOU THINKING WHEN YOU GOT DRESSED THIS MORNING?" Or "HEY, COULD YOU KEEP AT LEAST A HUNDRED POUNDS OF THAT STOMACH TO YOURSELF? WHAT PART OF THE WORD DIET DON'T YOU UNDERSTAND?"

I like to be surrounded by my own three feet of space as well as the next person, and I don't like having that space invaded on an elevator. In fact, I don't really want to get any closer to most strangers than an extended arm would allow. I've often thought that some people extend a hand for a handshake just to make sure certain people keep their distance.

Once I get on a crowded elevator, I adopt a defense described by author Dan Jenkins as one of the ten stages of drunkenness: becoming invisible. If I stand perfectly still and stare at the wall, I can pretend to be invisible and thus ignore the unwanted press of a stranger's body.

Talking on elevators also invites an intimacy that I don't want in a space I can't escape. It's one thing to talk to strangers at a cocktail party, or even a bus stop, because you can mill about or move away if you discover you've started a conversation with the subject of yesterday's "Serial Killer At Large" headline.

But there's no where to mill on an elevator. I'm stuck until it stops, and the best I can do is fantasize about the havoc I could create with my fellow captives if I drew them into a conversation. To the man pressing too close, even in a crowded elevator, I'd like to turn suddenly and say in a loud voice "THE RABBIT DIED, AND YOU'RE GOING TO DO THE RIGHT THING WHETHER YOU WANT TO OR NOT. AND I'M NOT TALKING ABOUT PAYING FUNERAL EXPENSES, EITHER."

And then there's always one person, male or female, who gets up in the morning and bathes in musk oil in the fervent hope that he or she can nauseate ten or fifteen people in an elevator. To that person I'd like to say "IF GOD WANTED YOU TO SMELL LIKE A MINK, HE WOULD HAVE GIVEN YOU A LITTLE FUR PELT WITH LITTLE TINY FEET TO GO WITH THOSE LITTLE TINY BEADY EYES. I HATE YOU AND EVERYBODY WHO SMELLS LIKE YOU, AND WHAT YOU ARE NOW ABOUT TO WITNESS IS CALLED MUSK-OIL INDUCED PROJECTILE VOMITING."

I got in a hotel elevator late one night in Chicago thinking I was alone. But as the doors began to close, I was startled to see Arte Johnson, one of the stars of the old *Laugh In* show, huddled in the corner with his back pressed against the wall. He looked at me with a weak smile and said "I don't like elevators." "I don't either," I said, retreating to the opposite corner.

We rode in silence; he looked at the floor and I looked at the wall. Maybe I should have asked him what fantasies he makes up about closed elevator doors.

Sleepless Nights

Ever since I was a kid, I've suffered sleep disorders of some kind—sleepwalking, nightmares, insomnia and/or talking in my sleep, which is a dangerous practice at times. My mother says it's hyperactive behavior—I lack the ability to shut down and turn my mind off. And, depending upon whatever other behavior she thinks I've been engaging in, she often mentions "no rest for the wicked."

Left to my own devices, I have the pulse rate of a hummingbird on acid. And despite all my best efforts, I usually go to bed telegraphing this message to the sandman: GET OUTTA HERE, I'M BUSY. I GOT STUFF TO DO. So, as the body is wont to do when sleep doesn't come easily, it finds a way to compensate.

What I have instead is a blessed gift—the ability to fall instantly into a deep sleep coma when trapped by boring situations. As a result, I slept through several years of church services, most of high school, a great deal of college and all of graduate school.

I had schoolsleep honed to perfection—I would stay awake for the first ten minutes—waving my hand wildly when the teacher asked questions, and when I was confident I'd created the perception that I was actively involved in class, I'd fall asleep. I'd sleep for a few seconds, or minutes, I could never tell the difference, and then I'd wake up, answer another question, and fall asleep again.

This technique worked especially well for English and American literature, history, political science and economics since most of what was required of me outside of class was reading. I truly excel at reading, and I've only slept through two books—*One Hundred Years of Solitude* and *The Name of The Rose.* Three years ago, however, when I went through a summer of chronic insomnia I discovered that the complete set of *The History of Civilization* by Will and Ariel Durant could put the over-the-counter sleeping pill companies permanently out of business.

But my schoolsleep technique literally failed me in math, and nearly failed me in Latin. I graduated from high school believing Euclidian Geometry was an avant garde wallpaper pattern, but I fully grasped the notion of *carpe diem.* And to this day, whenever my plane lands safely, I still reverentially whisper *terra firma.*

And they say the quality of education in this country is declining.

Churchsleep was easy to master, although I admit I suffered an impoverished spirit as a result. I was forced to find a discreet way to combat boredom in church since my early childhood methods—sneaking outside to play—were met with the paddle. Since I was conditioned to think of sermons as lectures, it was easy to fall asleep the instant the minister opened his mouth.

I've learned the hard way, though, that while boredom-sleep is a gift to me, and forgivable when I was a teen-ager, it is far more difficult to get away with as an adult.

But what I have learned, as an adult, is to make every effort to avoid those situations in which I know instant REM sleep will overtake me. The mere mention of chamber music, for example, makes my eyes glaze over, as does receiving an invitation to attend a seminar entitled "The Complete History of 'UH' As An Audible Pause."

But it is far more difficult to avoid boring people than it is to avoid boring situations. Boring people rarely announce themselves; they're just suddenly in your face haranguing you with missionary zeal about golf, or lawn care, or telling you about their latest support group, whether it's "Cellular Phone Addiction—Women Who Love Men Who Talk Too Much," or "Dance Fever—Stop Me Before I Two-Step Again."

I'd almost rather attend a lecture by George Bush on "Semantics Is Too A Foreign Language" than go to a cocktail party. For all my sleep-as-escape expertise, I've never yet been able to perfect sleepwalking while trying to make conversation with people I've never seen before and most likely will never want to see again. I just mentally slip into my alien role and think of all the new things I'll have to report when I return to my planet. While I heartily concur with Nietzsche's sentiment that life is a hundred times too short for us to bore ourselves, there is one good thing about going to a cocktail party: if death were to occur, the transition would be so subtle I'd never notice.

Pages To Paradise

In the event you ever decide to help yourself, there are thousands—perhaps millions—of self-help books on the market. I tried to help myself once and discovered that most self-help books are written by people who can't get a day job.

Huge numbers of these books are theoretical in nature—lacking in practical help for day-to-day living. It's hard to 'Take Control of Your Life' when the man sitting next to you on the bus takes out his false teeth and starts up a clacketyclack conversation in your ear. It's also hard to 'Turn Your Dreams Into Reality' when you're standing knee-deep in a flooded basement and your neighbor's 100-year-old oak tree is resting comfortably in the middle of your roof.

Because many of us need real help in a big way, I called my friend David, the psychiatrist, and asked him why no one writes books called 'How to Manage Bizarre Bus Incidents' or 'How to Turn Your Neighbor's Tree Into Firewood for Fun and Profit.'

"It's simple," he said. "No one would buy those books because we like to think we can get a grip on the larger, more cosmic issues in life. If we can enhance our self-esteem, pursue our true goals and improve the quality of our relationships, then the weirdos on the bus and the water in the basement and the tree on the roof become trivial problems that can easily be dealt with."

"Oh," I said. "Does this mean I have low self-esteem, don't know my goals from a hole in the ground and have lousy relationships because it unnerves me when people take their teeth out and play with them on the bus?"

"No, no," he assured me. "It just means that you've got a little more work to do. It's all a matter of perspective. These daily aggravations should simply be viewed as threads in the great tapestry of life."

"Do you actually charge people money for saying things like that?" I asked, incredulous. I was about to go on, but there was a distinct click on the other end.

Despite David's expansive pronouncements, I can't help but believe the self-help industry could do a better job for those of us on the edge of the ledge if they sought out books by people who were really capable of writing practical advice. Here are a few titles I'd like to see in the bookstore:

Have Fun At the Expense of Others by H. Ross Perot

How To Talk Without Moving Your Lips
by George Bush

Dating Tips by Justice Clarence Thomas

How To Host Large Gatherings
by Pope John Paul II

Say No And Mean It by Mario Cuomo

How To Have a Nice Day by Clint Eastwood

Powernaps—The Path To Success by Ronald Reagan

Making Stand-up Comedy Work For You
by Sen. Jesse Helms

What To Do If You Don't Like Your Nose by The Jacksons

Mommy's Special Cookie Secrets by Hillary Clinton

Counting Is Easier Than Spelling: Trickle Down Economics Explained by Dan Quayle

Write On

On those occasions when I'm not trying to bend the universe to my will in order to make a living, I often ponder the plight of the modern-day biographer. The exponential growth in communications technology has all but erased one of the biographer's most important tools—the personal letter.

Granted, my time might be better spent writing an article for *Family Circle* entitled '101 Ways to Extrude Macramé From Toxic Waste,' or trying to appease my mother by foraging for food with some redeeming nutritional value at least every eight days.

But the decline of the personal letter saddens me.

Where would the great biographies of Winston Churchill, Dorothy Parker and D.H. Lawrence be without the humanizing touch of their personal letters? Literature would suffer without the letters of George Sand and Gustave Flaubert, who revealed themselves to each other in a body of correspondence that stretched over a period of 12 years.

Could we really know Ernest Hemingway without

reading his letters?

Dear Mom,

It was a very good day. Went to the bullfights, spit a lot, killed three rhinos, drank four quarts of Scotch, ate nine dozen raw oysters, got another divorce.

Farewell,
Ernest

Now the personal letter has all but disappeared into the electronic abyss of fax machines, express mail, answering machines, overnight deliveries, voice mail, telegrams, computer bulletin boards and Post-It notes.

Formal business correspondence is often reduced to headlines that are faxed around the world in an instant:

Acme Bulbs, Holland

Please be advised that we ordered 100 dozen tulips—not juleps. We are not amused. Please re-ship immediately or we will instruct Margaret Thatcher to seize your country.

Regards,
The White House Garden Staff

Greeting-card companies make it even easier for us to avoid writing letters because they employ scores of writers who distill our thoughts and emotions, our love and our hate, into sentence fragments that can be purchased for a couple of dollars at the drugstore.

But I do have two friends in particular who easily find their voices in long letters and who write intimately and freely—unafraid of committing their thoughts to paper. One writes with thoughtful, wry humor from his own metaphysical point of view; the other writes exactly as he speaks to me—straight from the heart with daunting intelligence and merry British wit.

Letter-writing is not totally lost for me, either. I have

written letters full of joy and love, and I have written letters full of pain and sadness. Sometimes I write to entertain, sometimes to inform, and sometimes to say I'd be ever so pleased if the recipient were hit by a bus. But mostly I write because I simply need to confide in a close friend who is far away.

The key to honest expression is to write without censorship or fear, and without any worry about your letter ending up in someone's secret hiding place. Whatever feeling you have is valid at the time you have it. One of the most expressive letters I ever wrote consisted of two words; the instant it dropped into the slot I thought for sure I would regret it.

But I never did.

Even though greeting cards may be adding to the decline of the personal letter, I can't resist a card that instantly crystallizes or mirrors my feelings. I recently bought a card for someone I thought I knew well, a missive with a perfect message: "Your moon may be in Scorpio, but your head is in Uranus."

I think I'll fax it to him.

Even Wild Women
Get The Blues

One of my favorite books is *Infamous Women*, which I bought at the J.B. Speed Art Museum. Its pages are devoted to the lives and deaths of several colorful women, including Lucretia Borgia, Mata Hari, Empress Catherine the Great, and, of course, the wildly popular Joanna of Naples.

I like this book for several reasons, not the least of which is that it's written for the average eight-year-old. About Queen Isabella of England, the authors write, "In 1308, when Isabella was 12, her father King Philip IV of France, married her to King Edward II of England, who was 25. This was her bad luck."

No kidding.

I also like the book because it includes paper-doll cutouts of all the women it describes. Madame De Brinvilliers was rather attractive according to her paper doll likeness, but she had a bad habit of poisoning people who didn't give her what she wanted. Eventually she was hauled off in a dung cart to the chopping block where she was beheaded. Well, we all have our bad days.

As I was cutting out the Empress Wu paper-doll (she

killed three of her own children and most of her in-laws to get to the throne of China), it struck me that today's children have no record of the contemporary infamous women who have influenced their world. For the sake of historical accuracy, here are a few of my favorite infamous women of this century:

Panda Mae Sweetwater of Tupelo, Miss., awoke one morning feeling cross and grumpy and mean. As she stood at the kitchen counter rolling out the biscuit dough, her husband Alpo sneaked up behind her and kissed her on the back of the neck. Panda Mae turned and summarily dispatched Alpo with the rolling pin, then baked all the biscuits for herself. Panda Mae died of water retention in 1936, and since that time the shabby treatment of loved ones has been known as 'PMS,' or poor marital syndrome.

Blanche Stella of New Orleans, La., was the only secretary of transportation to declare the city's public conveyances off-limits to the visually unappealing. Blanche's brother, Stanley, was shocked by his sister's blatant discrimination and started his own enterprise, The Passion Train, which welcomed all passengers, especially those with fallen arches and excessively loose skin.

Sara Lee Crocker of Syracuse, N.Y., invented the cake mix in 1942 after taking a day job that kept her away from home in the afternoon when her family thought she should be preparing dinner. Sara Lee's jealous sister, Betty, took credit for the cake mix, as well as their Aunt Jemima's pancakes, and went off to live in Minneapolis. It's true that Betty achieved fame and fortune with her ill-gotten gains, but she was punished by having to live on a cardboard box, unfashionably coiffed in a weird hairdo now being copied by Marilyn Quayle.

Alitalia Quantas of Yankton, S.D., was the first person in her hometown to fly overseas in order to see a right-wing dictatorship close-up. Unfortunately, Alitalia forgot to check with her doctor about gamma globulin shots and tetanus boosters and was never heard from again, except for a postcard to her mother telling her that she thought she'd seen Ivan Boesky with dreadlocks.

Carlotta Cannoli of Brooklyn, N.Y., the first woman to be thought of by the current administration, was arrested recently for failing to disclose income her husband had received from baked goods. During the investigation, Carlotta's cousin, Geraldino, a TV reporter, uncovered a subversive plot to discredit croissants, sticky buns and artificial sweetener. At the hearing, Carlotta insisted that her husband's activities were neither covert nor illegal, and that his only politically motivated act was telling Albert Gore he'd look good as a *Solid Gold* dancer.

Tiffany Stepford of Dallas, Tx., was the first wife to perfect the forced smile, the air kiss and the empty gaze. Fed up after years of smiling through corporate cocktail parties and gazing adoringly at her husband, Tiffany checked herself into a hospital to have her jaw broken and her eyes tested. A few weeks later, wearing bifocals and a satisfied look, Tiffany planted a bomb in her husband's office and traded her inheritance for a nightclub with male dancers.

Food For Thought

Food is so 'in' now that even my former fast-food friends are turning into food snobs. One who used to serve Mrs. Paul's Fish Sticks at formal dinner parties now knows the secret to blackened redfish, and one who used to eat collard greens out of the can now adds myrrh to his Cream of Wheat. The one who would only eat beef that he killed himself with his knife and fork has turned into a devotee of midget vegetables and wheat germ. I still don't understand why anyone wants to eat germs that live in wheat.

I miss those nights when my friends and I used to get together and order out from Eat Pizza or Die and drink Moosehead—the only good green vegetable. I still remember a time when it was okay to eat pouch-food straight from the microwave and not have to apologize to anyone if they found a yellow box of cheese-like material in the fridge. Now I have to tell people that it belongs to my dog.

Mostly my friends just want to go to La Fern and drape their designer laps with pink napkins and eat foodette that costs a fortune.

I have this fantasy that I could open a restaurant called Casa Yo Mama, serve suckerfish at $40 a whack and the place would be surrounded with yupmobiles every night. If the dessert menu included gelato, particularly a flavor made from pure hazelnuts, the yups would go into a feeding frenzy.

At Casa Yo Mama lettuce would get washed only if it fell in the dishwater and the suckerfish would be blackened simply because the chef was a child of a depleted gene pool. But no matter—customers would line up around the block for the privilege of being turned away by a maitre d' who studied at the School of the Scornful Sneer.

His you're-not-fit-to-eat-here attitude would be rivaled only by that of the wine steward, who would know that on the willing-to-be-humiliated-by-restaurant-employee scale, food snobs can't hold a corkscrew to wine snobs.

Wine snobs put up with the officious wine steward because of the potential power they have to dismiss the proffered beverage. But almost unfailingly, after feeling the cork and ceremoniously swirling and tasting the wine, the wine snob pronounces it excellent and it's served all around. The food snob doesn't get to taste or feel the food first; he must simply pronounce it excellent without any ceremony.

This current fixation on cuisine is likely to cause a backlash that will seriously endanger the economic well-being of the fancy restaurants. People will tire of paying $20 for a mouse-size serving, and off they'll go to Kentucky Fried Chicken for a $3.39 plate of chicken and biscuits. Shortly thereafter, La Fern's catch-of-the-day will be Chicken Fried Swordfish.

We've already seen a foreshadowing of the lowest common denominator in the movie *Repo Man*, when the star goes to the refrigerator and eats from a can labeled 'Food.'

The Cost
Of Education

I recently noticed a comment attributed to Susie Tompkins, one of the co-founders of Esprit, who said, "These days, I think you feel incomplete if you buy and don't learn something." Tompkins was talking about corporate commitment to social and environmental issues, and the social contract that corporations maintain to provide information to their consumers.

Oh no, I thought, there goes the last of the feel-good experiences. Shopping is now like sex and relationships and career moves—part of the life experience we must evaluate, analyze and measure; selecting and rejecting experiences based on their worth as an opportunity to learn and/or grow.

Shopping always was an escape from mental hand-wringing; it was the last thing left that I could do without a rigorous test of my morality, my judgment, my sanity, my values or a note from my doctor. And the best part about shopping was that I didn't have to leave my house and wander around with strangers in that vast wasteland that frightens me so much—the shopping mall.

All I had to do was sit by the phone with a stack of

catalogs, put my feet up and knock myself out. And if I wanted to shop at 3 a.m., it was not only possible, it was easier because the phones were never busy. The only learning I had to do when I bought something was find the answer to the question "HAVE YOU LOST YOUR MIND? HOW ARE YOU GOING TO PAY FOR ALL THIS?"

But now I must learn something everytime I buy, or run the risk of feeling incomplete.

I am not having some fun now.

I tried to get in touch with the shopping/learning experience recently when I made my quarterly trip to the grocery store with my friend Vinnie. Right off the bat I learned that going to the grocery store at midnight on Saturday night is pretty cool because everyone else is out somewhere dealing with the Saturday night fun imperative.

Vinnie insisted on driving the cart, then abandoned me in Feminine Hygiene, picked me up in Produce, dumped me in Dairy Products, banged into me at The Bakery, and shouted instructions at me in Dog/Cat Food: "GET TORI SOME LOW FAT DOG FOOD, GOD KNOWS HE NEEDS IT AND HERE—GET A MUZZLE FOR THAT VICIOUS CAT; NO, NO, GET THIS—IT'S A GIANT RAT TRAP!"

I tried to explain to Vinnie that he was clouding up my learn-while-you-buy experience, but he was too busy drop-kicking frozen turkeys in Aisle 3 to pay attention. After wandering off alone in search of consumer knowledge, I picked up a bottle of vinegar with a bright red label containing the declaration "NOT MADE WITH PETROLEUM." What? Not made with petroleum? Does that mean I've been eating PETROLEUM VINEGAR

RIGHT UP TO THIS MINUTE? Does it mean it is now made with TOXIC WASTE? WHAT IF I WANT VINEGAR MADE WITH PETROLEUM? WHAT DO I DO THEN? IS THIS THE KIND OF THING I WANT TO LEARN WHEN I BUY A BOTTLE OF VINEGAR—THAT IT IS NOT MADE WITH PETROLEUM?

Vinnie careened around the corner, toppling an elderly shopper and a tower of canned peas, and skidded to a stop next to me. "WILL YOU KEEP YOUR VOICE DOWN?" he yelled. "WHY ARE YOU OVER HERE SCREAMING ABOUT PETROLEUM IN THE VINEGAR? YOU CAME HERE TO LEARN SOMETHING, AND THEN YOU GET MAD ABOUT IT. I CAN'T TAKE YOU ANYWHERE." And off he went again, burning cart rubber skid marks on the floor.

Great, I thought. This is just great. A shopping nightmare—I'll pick up a can of peas off the floor and it will say "JUST KIDDING, NOT MADE FROM PEAS AT ALL." Then I'll go back to the dairy case for a carton of cream and all the cartons will be labeled with "DIDN'T COME FROM REAL COWS, BUT HEY, NOT MADE WITH PETROLEUM EITHER." And, oh my God, the labels in the meat department: "WE'RE NOT SURE WHAT THIS IS, BUT DOES NOT CONTAIN NAUGAHYDE," or "ASSORTED RIBTIPS—NOT MADE WITH RAYON."

I dropped the bottle of vinegar and ran through the store looking for Vinnie. I found him at the greeting-card rack where he was busy switching all the cards. "Hi," he said, switching the "Happy Birthday From Your Son" cards with the "I Hate You and I Pawned Your Golf

Clubs" cards.

"Do you realize how long it's going to take people to find the right cards after you've moved them all around?" I said.

"Dealing with frustration is a good learning experience," Vinnie said, tidying up the Bar Mitzvah cards. "Speaking of frustration, have you worked through your fit of petroleum pique yet? Should we start a support group for the gastronomically disenfranchised? What have you learned here? HAVE YOU LEARNED ANYTHING AT ALL?"

"Yes," I said, wrestling the cart away from him. "The next time I want vinegar I'll get it at the gas station, and the next time I go out in public with you will be the day Megadeth is recorded on the Windham Hill label."

Deck Your Own Halls

Let's Talk Turkey

Even without looking at the calendar, I know Thanksgiving is only three weeks away. The same sixth sense that tells me an accident is about to happen foreshadows this traditional American family holiday and fills me with palpable anxiety.

This anxiety, Fear of Turkey (known to the medical community as Meleagris Gallopava Phobia), will not leave me until the day after Thanksgiving. Turkeyphobia seriously curtails my social activities. My friends invite me for Thanksgiving dinner, but I beg off, weakly pleading a case that my towels need rotating. I debate sending Miss Manners an emergency turkeygram:

Dear Miss Manners:

Is it bad form to ask your friends right up front if they're serving turkey on Thanksgiving? Could I accept an invitation for Thanksgiving dinner and then eat everything else except the dead bird? Could I, a known devotee of steak tartare, get away with a sudden declaration that I've become a vegetarian?

These hard-sought answers are difficult to come by, and

the situation remains delicate. I continue to decline these invitations, and my friends now suspect that I engage in some anti-American activity on Thanksgiving Day. But the truth is, Thanksgiving is my favorite holiday. It's warm and convivial, and except for the turkey, the house smells good. People get together for a good time and don't feel compelled to spend hundreds of dollars giving each other presents they don't like. The only thing wrong with Thanksgiving is that people do feel compelled to eat turkey. Americans are big on tradition, and I give the New England colonists all the credit in the world for finding the wild turkey in the forest. They got lost trying to find the Kroger Superstore and they did the best they could. But I wish they had run across a slightly more attractive or intelligent food to serve on that first Thanksgiving Day.

The real problem I have with turkey is that it bears too much resemblance to the turkey vulture to suit my taste. Every time I see the turkey glowing in the middle of the table, fairly bursting with juice under the carving knife, I wonder if it had its last meal on the side of the road.

I'm also confused by the other food we eat on Thanksgiving and don't see again until next year. I have a vision of canning factories lying fallow and choking with dust until mid-November. Suddenly they crank up with ear-splitting intensity and for days churn out billions of cans of cranberry sauce. Then on Thanksgiving Eve they shudder to a halt and spin cobwebs for another year.

Why don't we eat cranberry sauce on Sept. 11? Or the Fourth of July? And if dressing were good for us, why wouldn't we eat it more than once a year? I'd like to know who thought up dressing anyway. Dressing is deep-fried shag carpet.

Two years ago I tried to exorcise this Fear of Turkey by going through the cooking ritual myself. I asked one of my cooking friends where I could go to buy a turkey. Then I asked another one of my cooking friends how to cook it. Then I asked my family and a few of my more adventuresome friends to come by and eat it. My family was pleased about this sudden leap forward into domesticity, but my friends were filled with dread. But that's what friends are for.

I thought things were going rather well until my father gently suggested that turkey is best presented without the little plastic bag of assorted body parts inside. One of my former friends, not nearly so forgiving of my faults as my father, rather harshly suggested that turkey is also best presented well-done, as opposed to rare.

My aunt then took note of the fact that I use my oven as storage for unused pot and pans, and asked me if I had simply let the turkey sit in the rather pale fall sun for a few hours. Having been reared with good social-grace notes, and taught to have deference and respect for one's elders, particularly when they are family, I suggested in my most genteel fashion what they could all do with the little bleeding beast.

Time heals even turkey wounds, and once again I expect to be in the warm circle of family and friends for Thanksgiving dinner. Well, almost in the circle. Mother said if I promised never to cook a turkey again, I could have fried chicken and sweet-potato pie. All to myself.

Deck Your Own Halls

I f you didn't participate last month in America's most gruesome blood sport—Christmas-shopping on the day after Thanksgiving—I suspect you suffer, as I do, from CMMGS (Christmas Makes Me Grumpy Syndrome).

I love Christmas, but the fa-la-la that surrounds it makes me bristle: I hate to shop, eggnog makes me want to put my thumb in someone's eye, and I get tired of the Christmas decorations that have been on display ever since the summer clearance sales. I'm also reasonably sure I still won't get a pony.

What makes most of us CMMGS sufferers grumpy is the long list of things we have to do before Christmas even gets here. But I've made an early New Year's resolution that this Christmas will be different; it will be a kinder and gentler Christmas, more focused on real values—like how little effort I can expend and not alienate my family and friends to the point where they won't buy me presents.

If you'd like a simpler, merrier Christmas without much fuss, I have a few ideas for you:

Even under the best of circumstances, Christmas is a stressful time, and the constant round of parties and rich food requires a good deal of physical stamina and fitness. It's not too late to take up running; in the next couple of weeks, make it a point to run to the table at mealtime, run to the phone in case it's an invitation to a party, and take those stairs two at a time when you realize you've left your cigarettes in the bedroom.

A positive attitude is extremely important during the holidays. Stand in front of the mirror and practice exclaiming, "Oh, you shouldn't have! I love it! Does the surplus store accept returns on irregular merchandise?" Or, "Oh, what a good friend you are. How could you have possibly known that my record collection would never be complete without Lawrence Welk's *Little-Known Ukranian Reggae Polka Hits?* I know you'll just love the macramé underwear I got you."

Sending Christmas cards is both time-consuming and expensive. If you don't have the courage to just say no, then cut down gradually. First eliminate your closest personal friends. Since you see them all year long, just make a note to wish them a Merry Christmas personally on a quarterly basis.

If you absolutely must send cards to your out-of-town friends, save yourself a dime by sending them a postcard, and tell them you hope they have Merry Christmases for as long as they live because this is absolutely the last time they'll hear from you.

For the people on your list you despise, send a long, chatty Christmas newsletter detailing every inane thing that you, or your family, your friends and your pets have done since last Dec. 26. Pay particular attention to digestive-tract illnesses, oral hygiene and brake alignments.

The best way to reduce your Christmas stress is to eliminate all Christmas shopping. Sit down and make the list as if you were actually going to go out and buy presents. Then burn the list and sit quietly for 10 minutes. If the paroxysms of guilt do not send you into total paralysis, you are either a cold, heartless person or a Virgo. In either case, you are now free to spend all that money on yourself, like Geminis do all year long. If the guilt is too much for you, compromise. Convert to Judaism, or send your friends and family this note:

"Dear One,

"I've just had an out-of-body experience that has left me in an altered state of consciousness. I hope you understand that this condition has rendered me unable to go out and buy you the usual six or eight wildly extravagant Christmas presents that I would have bought under normal circumstances. The big jolly doctor told me I could expect a complete recovery around midnight on Christmas Eve—provided, of course, that I remain calm and stop trying to escape. But it's not all bad here at Twilight Gardens. I like Rudolph a lot, but honestly, Dancer and Prancer get on my nerves standing around in front of the mirror all day.

"Well, I have to go now. It's time for my favorite activities—naps and Mr. Medication.

"Much love to you all, and Merry Christmas."

Have An
Extended Christmas

Christmas shopping is a breeze for my friend Larry because he doesn't buy presents for anybody except his girlfriend. I once assumed this shopping shortfall had to do with his religious beliefs, since he converted to Judaism. But no, he says, it's just that every year his Christmas list got longer and longer and more expensive and more complicated and he just suddenly said no.

I don't think that would work for me, even though I do wish Christmas were simpler than it is now. It was pretty simple when I was a kid. I bought presents for my sister, my mom and dad, my only set of grandparents, and Sylvester, the cat. On those rare occasions when I was in good graces at school, I would buy my favorite teacher a gift, but only if my mother made me. I had pretend presents for my imaginary friend, Barry, and my boon companion, Denny the bear.

When I was in high school, I had the same list, but added to it my best girlfriends and whatever boyfriend happened to be in vogue at the time. When I went to college, I included my college roommate, and since no professor ever looked upon me with favor, I dropped teachers and added my sister's husband to the family list.

After I got married, I wisely replaced my boyfriends with my husband, added his family (my mother made me), dropped my high school friends and my college roommate off the list, and added two dogs to the aging Sylvester.

Then I got a divorce, lost my grandparents, my sister had a daughter, Sylvester deleted himself, I kept the dogs, and it became no longer socially acceptable to have an imaginary friend or a boon bear companion.

So my Christmas list had expanded and contracted again to family, close friends and pets—except on those rare occasions when I was in good graces with my boss, at which time I would add him to the list, but only if my secretary made me.

Now that I'm on my own, business gift giving is at a minimum, so I concentrate on my family, my closest friends, my dog and cat, people whose services I use regularly, and all the 'Dear Santa' letters I can take from the post office without suffering fatal heartbreak.

As long as my Christmas list is, and as much money as it takes to get through Christmas, I still consider myself lucky when I think about the expense and complications that blended and extended families face at Christmas.

The simple nuclear family unit of old—Mom, Dad, Jane, Dick, Spot and Puff—has given way to a blinding assortment of ex-wives, ex-husbands, stepchildren, step-parents, half-stepparents, multiple godparents, and a dizzying array of mammaws and pawpaws.

With wild abandon, the new wives and husbands blend new children, old children, stepchildren, new in-laws, old in-laws, new friends, old friends, new and old mammaws and pawpaws, and his-and-her lovers.

Some of these extended and blended families approximate the population of Rhode Island, and any single person who lives next door runs a real risk of being sucked into the vortex. Try explaining to one of these families that one of the principal benefits of living alone is that you don't have to wake up in the arms of a loved one.

Even poor Spot and Puff realize with horror that the new wife/husband/stepdaughter/stepson has dragged in step-pets, and now they have to share their pitiful cellophane-pet Christmas stockings with Checkers and Whiskers and Huffywuffy.

But I must go now. President Bush just called, and in the spirit of the ongoing federal budget reduction, he asked me to write a Christmas gift-giving guide for his extended family entitled *How To Get Through Christmas on $50,000.00 A Day.*

You'd Better Not Cry

was in a cafe recently, having an adult beverage with some friends, when I noticed an extremely attractive older man sitting alone at the bar. I've had the good fortune to see extremely attractive older men out alone before, but this one was particularly noteworthy. He had a long list and he appeared to be checking it twice. And he was wearing red pajamas.

I know that some men actually wear pajamas because my friend May Lee swears she was present during a live pajama performance. But then May Lee lives in Montgomery, Ala., where pajama-wearing is probably another venerable Southern custom. Anyway, I've never been able to resist a trap door, so I went over to say hello.

"Hello," I said. "I couldn't help but notice that you're an extremely attractive older man sitting here alone at the bar wearing your jammies. Couldn't you sleep? Do you live in Montgomery? And what's this list that you appear to be checking twice? Is it your grocery list?"

"My, aren't we the inquisitive one?" he said, peering at me over the tops of his little rimless glasses. "And why are you squinting? Do you have something in your eye?"

"No, it's just that the twinkle in your eye is so bright it's blinding me."

"Ho, ho, ho," he boomed. "You really don't know who I am, do you?"

"Well, you do look awfully familiar," I said. "And there's something about you that makes me want to hug people and wish them peace on earth and good will toward men. Not to mention women and children. Are you St. Teddy the Bear?"

"Something like that," he said, suddenly sad. "You see, I remember a time not so long ago when everyone knew me and looked forward to that one time of year when I would come to visit and leave little tokens of the good will that you spoke about."

"What happened? Why did people forget you? And why did you suddenly get sad?" I asked.

"Because these little tokens of good will turned into a multi-billion-dollar seasonal industry, and because parents have taught their children that a present is nothing unless it can walk and talk and drive little cars and shoot lasers and cost hundreds of dollars."

"You see, I used to fill up my sleigh with candy and fruit and sweet little rag dolls and toy trucks and the spirit of love and friendship. My tiny reindeer team could easily haul the load. But if this keeps up," he said, eyeing his list, "I'll have to turn the reindeer out to pasture and rent an 18-wheeler."

I looked at his list. Designer clothes, mini-camcorders, car telephones, gold earrings, trips to Disneyland and the book, *How to Make a Million in Kindergarten*, by Sam Walton. There wasn't a sweet little rag doll or toy truck in sight.

"All these things are for the kids?" I asked in amazement. "Most adults I know don't have these things. Well, maybe they have Sam's book, but whatever happened to enough love and friendship to last us a whole year until you come again?"

"Yes, indeed," he said, the twinkle returning to his bright blue eyes. "And if you remember who I am, perhaps others will, too. Now if you'll excuse me, I have to go fill up my sleigh with candy and fruit and little rag dolls and toy trucks." He crumpled up the list and left it on the bar.

Then he turned to me at the door and said, "In the future, be more careful when you talk to extremely attractive older men sitting alone at the bar. They may be wearing their pajamas for an entirely different reason. Ho, ho, ho. Mer-ry Christmas."

Yes, indeed, Santa. And a Merry Christmas to you, too.

All I Want For Christmas

Dear Santa,

I know it's a little late to be writing you, but, to be honest, I'm still a little peeved about last Christmas. I thought the PITBULL-O-GRAM was a great way to get even with people who've been really bad, and I'm certain it would have been cheaper than stuffing coal in their stockings. I know you have an image to maintain, but it seems to me that a PITBULL-O-GRAM would be a pretty effective way to encourage better behavior; and it's so simple—you just ring the bad person's doorbell, cheerfully announce that you're delivering a PITBULL-O-GRAM, and then throw the dog inside and run.

You also hurt my feelings when you summarily rejected my suggestion that you send Dancer and Prancer to separate schools. I know they're just good friends, but they haven't been separated since birth, and I have to tell you there are a lot of people out there thinking, you know, well, Dancer's okay, but Prancer's co-dependent. And I swear I thought you already knew about Rudolph's speeding ticket. I was only trying to help, okay?

Listen, I hope you're not still mad at the monks; I didn't mean to let that slip, either. But if everyone else in the world is cashing in on Christmas, what's wrong with the monks selling fruitcakes? Talk about time on your hands. If you had to get up at 3:15 every morning like the monks do, you'd probably want to make fruitcakes too. I mean, how many times can you sweep a monastery?

Okay, okay, I know I owe you an explanation about the elves. I know I should have asked first, but I just wanted to borrow them for a little while. It was my annual 'Don't Worry—Elvis Is Still Dead' party, and I just thought they'd like to get out and kick up their little heels for awhile. I meant to get them back before their bedtime, but, boy those little guys can party hearty. They really don't get out much, do they? Anyway, I know you didn't get much out of them for a few days because they were all Grumpy, Cranky, Sleepy, Whiny, Dopey, etc., and I promise not to do it again. But, really, Wheezy's Elvis the Elf impersonation is just too cool for school. Those little blue-suede boots with the turned-up toes...

I re-read the letter you wrote me last year, and I have to agree that, once you got a grip on yourself, you made some good points. You're right—I was the one who should stop whining about not being able to find a Halloween costume for all the Christmas merchandise. Next year, I'll just dress up as a dead poinsettia.

Of course I still love Christmas as much as always, and I don't know where I ever got the idea that spending a lot of money is what Christmas is all about. Like you said, I sure didn't get it at home. When my sister, Carol, and I were kids, Christmas meant the one thing we wanted more than anything—the bicycle, the doll, or the BB gun, and a little mountain of wonderful things that didn't cost much— fuzzy mittens and bunny earmuffs and jacks and yo-yos and candy and books. But speaking of the one thing I always wanted more than anything—whatever happened to Tony the Pony? I never did get over that.

But I guess you never got over the Super Santa Sugar Snacks we used to leave for you on Christmas Eve, either. For a long time we thought you really liked them, then we figured out why we had to peel the poor dog off the ceiling on Christmas morning. He was the one who ate all the Chocolate Fudge With White Sugar Cookie Sandwiches we made for you. WE WERE JUST KIDS, OKAY? WHAT DID WE KNOW?

Remember when Carol and I used to lie in bed on Christmas Eve, wide awake but still as mice, fairly bursting with excitement while we waited for you to come? Then sure enough, late at night, we'd hear noises in the living room—the crunch of paper and ribbon, soft laughter, and the round rumble of a big, deep voice that was trying hard to be quiet.

The fragrance of strong, hot coffee and oranges and cinnamon and cloves drifted upstairs to our room, and I couldn't stand it any longer and I'd jump out of bed and run to Carol and say, "He's here! Santa Claus came!"

And Carol would hug me and say "Yes, he's here. Santa Claus always comes."

Merry Christmas, Santa.

Love,
Bonnie

Santa Answers
My Christmas Letter

SANTA CLAUS
#8 Reindeer Road
North Pole

Dear Bonnie,

Merry Christmas to you, too, and thank you for your long letter. Although I received your letter in the middle of August (my very first of the season, I believe), I can barely keep up with my shopping at this time of year, much less answer the mail. And to make matters worse, Rudolph turned 16 in November and now the sleigh is never around when I need it. Boys! I never had this much trouble when Dancer and Prancer learned to drive.

But never mind; being a parent is hard, but at least that's one problem you don't have. Anyway, your letter was of great interest to me, and I have some time to answer it now (Rudolph's driving the sleigh tonight; I think he's taking his girlfriend to see the Reindeer Games).

First, I'll try to address your complaint about the ever-extending holiday season. Yes, I know it's getting longer and longer and it makes me cranky as well. I'm aware that you couldn't even find a Halloween costume among all the Christmas decorations, but I'm at a loss to explain it myself—it's certainly not my doing. Personally, I'd like for Christmas to last two days—Christmas Eve and Christmas Day. Christmas Eve is the real magic to me—I love the anticipation and the excitement that make the little children fairly burst, and then to see their faces on Christmas morning! It makes me forget my aching back and how upset I was when the stores start promoting Christmas before the fall even started.

But what I suggest is that you simply ignore the commercial pressures. Just let the Christmas spirit come to you in its own time; and when it does, try to remember that Christmas was meant to be about love, not about how much you spend.

While I do agree with you about the length of the season, I don't agree that jolliness is an unnatural state. You may be right that some people can only achieve jolliness through various mood-altering devices, but I can assure you that it's easy to be jolly when just the mention of my name brings smiles to the faces of children around the world.

I do admit, however, that my jolliness disappears when I get letters from kids who want everything. But it's not their fault; they're used to getting everything they want, and I guess their parents have never told them about all the children who never have a single toy, or even a hug, on Christmas morning.

But that's why I have helpers out there, people like you and thousands of others who go to the post office at Christmas and help Santa out with his letters. (I appreciate your help, and I don't mean to criticize, but I thought your reply was a little over the top to the woman who wanted a new Firebird to give her boyfriend when he got out of jail).

To answer another question: no, we don't have a Christmas Union, although sometimes I think it might be a good idea. Frankly, it seems that I do most of the work, and I have to fly coach around the world. Frosty The Snowman never has to work in the Tropics, or anywhere in the South, and of course, Scrooge never works at all.

But honestly, I have no complaints because I've got the best job in the world, and the benefits are great. According to my contract, I'm guaranteed eternal life and perfect health; I'm ageless and changeless and I never have to worry about what to wear. Adults and children alike around the world love and adore me, I get to travel a lot, I have plenty of help (the elves just can't do enough, and they're such a joy—they're so, well, so *elfin*). And after I met Mrs. Claus at that Christmas Singles Toy Workshop, well, life is about as good as it gets. Rudolph's adolescence is a pain, but, as your mother would say, he'll get over it.

And, to answer your last question: Yes, it makes me sad that Christmas is a depressing time for so many people, but as your favorite philosopher, Doodah, would say, it does no good when we fall into the abyss of sadness because there is so much pain in the world. Good comes when we are aware of the pain, and then simply try to ease it in whatever way we can among those we find in our own path. That is the way for all of us to have a Merry Christmas.

Love,

Santa

P.S. If I were you, I'd buy my Halloween costume on Valentine's Day.

Yo, New Year

For the last 10 years I've made the same list of hopelessly unattainable New Year's resolutions: Save $85, put someone else's interests above my own at least once, lose two pounds, attend Easter services regularly, take the dog to the car wash for a bath in August, don't cheat in the grocery express lane, replace dead shrubs instead of spray-painting them green.

A year later, I always find the list at the bottom of a stack of cat-hair-covered clothes, warm thank-you notes from every major bank card and another list of 'Great Classics I Plan to Rewrite'. Just as I'm about to plunge into a few seconds of well-deserved guilt and despair over my inability to improve myself, my ego demands to know:

"Why do you make these stupid resolutions in the first place? Think of all the time you save checking out $60 worth of groceries in the express lane. And every year you save almost $85 by spraying your dead shrubs green. And remember that time you tried to help the pregnant woman who was stuck in a snowbank? It's not your fault it took two hours for the tow truck to show up. You don't need resolutions; you're perfect."

"Oh, sure," I say. "If I were a letter, I'd be marked 'return to sender'. If I were a bath towel, I'd be sold on a table marked 'highly irregular'. But you're right about one thing. Why make these self-defeating resolutions at all? Why not just resolve to live with my faults, and from now on focus the need for improvement where it belongs— squarely with someone else?"

Having cheerfully accepted my shortcomings as interesting personality disorders, I face the new year with a clear conscience and a few suggestions:

Airlines should resolve to look up the definition of food in the dictionary: "any substance that can be taken into the body of an animal or plant to maintain its life and growth." Nowhere—I repeat, nowhere—do the words "replica," "plastic," "foam rubber" or "Play Doh" appear in that definition.

Bill Cosby should resolve to spend some of his millions buying back his plotless TV shows.

David Brinkley should resolve to take a lesson from Sylvester Stallone: When you've told everything you know at least three times, a simple "Yo" will suffice.

Restaurant owners should resolve to insist that servers not remove plates until everyone at the table is finished eating. If you're the only person left with a plate, you feel like the last pig at the trough.

President Bush should resolve to become a Jeopardy contestant: "Most embarrassing vice presidents for $100, please, Alex."

Ted Turner should produce a new TV movie: "David Duke: A Political Portrait of the Spiritual Equivalent of Rock City."

Let's Get Personal

What We Have Here Is...

I was surprised to hear recently that one of my best friends is about to get married. I don't have anything against marriage; after all, it is a good way to meet people. But what surprised me is that I heard the news of the impending marriage from someone else.

Maybe my friend didn't tell me himself because he suspected I'd have dissident views on the subject. Or maybe he kept it to himself because he's using the next few months to practice up on non-communication techniques. All of us who've been married know that the first rule of marriage is to non-communicate with each other.

If you've somehow managed to escape marriage so far, the rules of marital non-communication are highly specific and written into the marriage ceremony: "Do you, Spike and Fluffy, promise to love and honor each other for so long as you both shall live? And do you both promise that you will never, ever tell the truth, or anything remotely resembling the truth about the way you really feel about anything?"

Spike and Fluffy solemnly promise.

Having so sworn to keep their true feelings to themselves, Spike and Fluffy set the stage for the three most-often-repeated words in the history of marriage:

"What's wrong?"

"Nothing."

Or, if one of them is feeling particularly chatty, the conversation might go like this:

"Is something bothering you?"

"No."

"Look, I know something's bothering you because you haven't spoken to me since the wedding reception, you wrote three checks to a private investigator, you sent the kids to boarding school in a foreign country and you put the house up for sale. Now tell me what's wrong."

"Nothing."

"Oh, good. I was getting a little worried."

Variations on this theme can hold the marriage together for another nine years. Then one day Fluffy announces:

"Look, I'm sick and tired of discussing this. I want a divorce."

So Spike and Fluffy get a divorce, but marital non-communication is so pervasive that the divorce court can't communicate either. The court can't say, "Spike and Fluffy were two perfectly nice people who happened to be totally unsuited for each other, and isn't it too bad they couldn't work it out? But aren't we pleased as can be that they didn't kill each other, and isn't it nice the kids are adjusting so well to their ex-patriot status at such a tender age?"

No. The divorce court maintains only that the marriage is "irretrievably broken." What was it—a vase? I remember looking up those words and imagining my grandad saying to my grandmother, "Lee, our granddaughter just broke this vase that's been in the family for about a thousand years. I believe it is irretrievably broken."

Anyway, non-communication does serve a purpose because it can keep the marriage together for what may seem like several lifetimes. Communicating your true feelings is no guarantee that the marriage will be happier or last longer:

"What's wrong?"

"What's wrong? You want to know what's wrong? Here's what's wrong. For starters, you're an insensitive, unsupportive, egomaniacal jerk. You never help around the house, you're never here when the kids get sick, you insult my mother, you kissed my best friend for three minutes and 14 seconds on New Year's Eve, you took the dog to the vet and you never brought him back, and you think Bobby Knight is a real swell guy. I hate you and everybody who looks like you."

"I see. Thank you for sharing that with me. Perhaps I'll go down to the corner bar and reflect on that for a few hours. I will return in the event I decide to integrate this constructive criticism into positive behavior modification."

Who Wrote The Book Of Love?

Over dinner recently, my friend Martini and I were engaged in an animated discussion of the ever-popular question, "What could she possibly see in him?" When she abruptly changed the subject.

"What's wrong, Mart?" I asked with real concern. Normally this debate about species attraction provides hours of relief from the more compelling issues of homelessness, world hunger and the true definition of *viscose.*

"The fact is, it's none of our business what they see in each other," she said flatly. "Who has any right to judge where matters of the heart are concerned?"

I was stunned. "Martini, you've just denied human beings one of their inalienable rights—the right to pass judgment on an individual's choice of a significant other. Everyone I know—including you, my mother and the parking lot attendant—has seen fit to give me the full benefit of your ill-formed and unwanted opinions about every relationship I've ever had. Why must I, all of a sudden, withhold an opinion in the face of what is clearly a marital accident waiting to happen?"

"Stop shredding your napkin," Martini said patiently. "It's just that you so obviously need help. You clearly know nothing about choosing a mate."

"A MATE?" I shouted. "If I wanted a mate, I'd go live in the zoo. Who do you think I am—Cheetah? And look who's talking: the 'Divorce Poster Girl' of the decade."

"Keep your voice down," Martini pleaded. "No wonder I hate having a meal with you in public. You attract the same attention as a public hanging or a multiple-car pileup. Besides, we're talking about you, not me. The fact that I've had a few marital mishaps is irrelevant."

"Record-breaking more accurately describes it," I said, making a desperate attempt to flag down a waiter bent upon ignoring us. "And who made up the rules of this conversation? Why are we only talking about me, not you? I'm not the one who got married a year ago because I didn't know how to use a self-service gas pump."

"Please don't set the tablecloth on fire," Martini begged. "I'm certain the waiter will come now that you've so neatly stacked all the dishes on the edge of the table. He wouldn't be ignoring us in the first place if you hadn't insisted he bring us a six-pack when he offered the wine list."

"I was just trying to save him some steps. He obviously doesn't keep up with the latest time-and-motion studies. Now could we please focus this discussion where it belongs—talking about one of our best friends behind her back? I'm really afraid Jo Ella is going to marry this geek."

"Oh, geek schmeek," Martini said. "You couldn't tell a geek from a Smurf. Your definition of a geek is any man who..."

"Please, spare me," I interrupted, snaring the waiter by the coattail. "Excuse me," I said to him. "Would it be possible for you to remove these disgusting dishes, bring us two cups of coffee and then submit your resignation to management effective immediately? Thank you."

"And now," I said, turning my attention back to Martini, who was trying to crawl under the table, let's be done with this fascinating litany of my shortcomings and get back to business. I could give you a dozen reasons why Jo Ella shouldn't marry Mars..."

"It's Lars, not Mars," Martini interjected. "If you're going to criticize him, you could at least get his name right."

"Okay, fine. Then that's the first thing wrong with him—Jo Ella doesn't know his name. She always calls him Mars, probably because that's his country of origin. Did you know he's trying to recreate his dead cat in a Petri dish, and that he can't read without using his finger? Talk about a chromosome recession, what we have here is a failure to trickle down..."

"So he's not perfect," Martini said. "You still have no right to judge. You don't know what needs he fulfills for Jo Ella, and at least give him credit for having a steady job, something our poor waiter no longer has, thanks to you."

"Speaking of the waiter," I said as I picked up the check, "why don't we introduce him to Jo Ella? He may not have a job anymore, but I really like a man who knows how to get even. Here, you pay this time. It's only $450."

Go To Jail

rvin R. Hertzel, a mathematician at Iowa State University, figured out there are 10 spaces on the Monopoly game board that a player will land on more than the others. This information intrigued me a great deal; perhaps it was because I, like Irvin, was having a slow day.

Nonetheless, the ten most landed-on squares are Go, Illinois Avenue, B&O Railroad, Tennessee Avenue, New York Avenue, Reading Railroad, St. James Place, Water Works, Pennsylvania Railroad and Free Parking.

What intrigues me is that a scholarly mathematician devoted his skill and expertise to discovering where we are most likely to land when we play Monopoly. But his findings also confirm my belief that the games we play mimic our behavior in life: Don't we start at Go when we're born, and occupy Free Parking when we die?

Anyway, Dr. Hertzel got all the attention and glory for having solved the Monopoly problem, and no one paid any attention to my friend Martini's mathematical breakthrough on a real-life game called Monogamy. Had you paid attention, you might not be in the middle of a messy divorce right now.

After years of experience and extensive research, Martini carefully constructed an elegant algorithm that makes Euclidian geometry look like toast.

Martini's Monogamy Algorithm, like all good algorithms, replaces all free variables with a specific number:

First, Martini counted the number of letters in her name—7.

She added the number of times she's been married—5.

She added the number of times she's been separated—11.

She added the number of times she's been divorced—4.

She added the number of marriages still intact—1.

She subtracted the number of times she regretted having said "I do"—5.

She added the number of times her husbands fooled around with other women—32.

She subtracted the number of times her husbands said, "But, sweetheart, it had nothing to do with you, I swear. It just happened."—32.

Finally, Martini added the number of times she's reflected on the simple perfection of a celibate, monastic existence—32.

Martini consulted her horoscope, briefly considered the notion that the cruelest lies are often told in silence, then solved the equation $(7+5+11+4+1-5+32-32+32)$ and found that her Emotional IQ equals 55.

Then Martini calculated her chances for true love in a monogamous relationship by multiplying her Emotional IQ (55) by the number of times she's been divorced (4); she subtracted this number, 220, from Fred Wiche's Down-Home Index, which is also 220, and ascertained that her chances for true love in a monogamous relationship are zero.

Having determined that her present husband is also a skilled practitioner of Propositional Calculus, Martini gave me a copy of a letter she plans to send to Dr. Hertzel:

Dear Dr. Hertzel,

The quality of my life has improved significantly since I now understand the overall probabilities associated with landing on each of the 40 squares on the Monopoly game board. Since you appear to have a fair amount of free time on your hands, I wonder if you could calculate for me the probability of drawing the Go To Jail card when one decides to take a Chance on tying one's husband to the tracks of the Pennsylvania Railroad?

Mind If I Play Through?

I've just finished reading a book about why men and women don't understand each other. The reason men and women don't understand each other is because we can't talk to each other, and the reason we can't talk to each other is because we don't speak the same language.

I knew that.

According to the book, much of our inability to talk to each other as adults has to do with how we learned to play as children. Boys start out playing games that have winners and losers, thus laying the groundwork for a hierarchal way of thinking: Am I winning or losing, am I one-up or one-down? Girls are more likely to play socially interactive games that don't necessarily create winners or losers, and thus tend to evaluate relationships based on whether they are creating intimacy or distance.

Therefore, when men and women talk about something of real significance, it is largely hopeless unless they make allowances for the fact that they are each trying to satisfy a completely different agenda. The male is always wondering whether he is winning or losing, and the female is always wondering if they are getting closer together or

218

farther apart.

Like most everyone else who's learned anything about mingling with the other species, I learned what little I know the hard way, but I'm happy to share it with you:

Men can tell you what they're thinking, but never ask them what they're feeling because (a) they don't know, and (b) they don't want to talk about it. But it is incorrect to assume that men don't have feelings. I know for a fact this is not true. Men have plenty of feelings. I was assured of this when I made my first and last appearance on a golf course with a man who was, at that time, my husband.

Since it seemed logical to me that the only purpose of using a golf cart was to get as close to the ball as possible, and since the only thing about golf that appealed to me was driving the golf cart, I drove the golf cart onto the green, stopping right beside the golf ball. Although some fairly cataclysmic feelings erupted instantly in my husband, I decided not to ask him about his feelings. Instead, I correctly asked him what he was thinking: "Spike, are you thinking about divorce?" As it turns out, he was not. He was thinking about murder.

We had now laid a foundation for a meaningful exchange of ideas, and the next logical step was to frame a question in such a way that it could be answered with yes or no: "Spike, the price you pay for murder is the irrevocable loss of someone you love, and, of course, the loss of your personal freedom for the rest of your life. Isn't that too high a price to pay for killing someone for simply driving a golf cart on the green?" Not at all, he said. In fact, it sounded like a pretty good deal.

The situation might appear tricky to those uninitiated in understanding the opposite sex, but I thought it was all going rather well. Five minutes had elapsed and I was still breathing.

Buoyed by the fact that I was getting straightforward answers to my questions, I ventured further afield: "Spike, don't you remember promising to love and honor me when we got married?" No, he said. He didn't remember that part. But he did recall something about the death part.

The situation seemed to be worsening, so I made one last ditch attempt at reconciliation and understanding in a final appeal based on logic, intellect and reason:

"I HATE THIS STUPID GAME, I HATE YOU AND I HATE YOU FOR MAKING ME PLAY IT, AND I HATE EVERYONE ELSE WHO PLAYS IT AND I HATE ALL THESE UGLY STUPID GREEN AND PINK CLOTHES EVERYBODY WEARS AND IF YOU COME NEAR ME I'LL HIT YOU WITH THIS STICK."

"It's not a stick, it's a three-iron," Spike said between clenched teeth.

"I DON'T CARE WHAT IT IS," I screamed. "GET AWAY FROM ME. I'D RATHER BE DEAD THAN BE MARRIED TO YOU."

"That can be arranged," he said, advancing toward me with a vein pulsating dangerously in his temple.

"YEA!" shouted a cheering foursome behind us. "DO WHATEVER YOU WANT, JUST GET THE STUPID CART OFF THE GREEN."

Divided We Stand

My friend Patrick observed the other day that the dividing line between men and women is the Three Stooges. He contends that if the Three Stooges suddenly appeared on TV, all the men in the room would be riveted to the screen and all the women would leave.

Patrick argues that the Three Stooges appeal to men because they are simple-minded, superficial and violent. He says they lack the subtlety, finesse and layers of emotional depth that appeal to women.

I disagreed, since my favorite Breakfast of Champions consists of eating a meatloaf sandwich while watching the Three Stooges at 7 a.m. on cable TV. I am particularly fond of Larry, the one whose hair fluffs up wildly around his ears; I suspect he also lived in an area where the relative humidity is always 100 percent.

Anyway, this discussion caused me to devote considerable thought to the question of what really divides men and women these days. This would have been a much easier question to answer before the women's movement ushered in the kicking and screaming sensitive male.

And it was an easy question to answer when I was growing up. My dad was the one with short hair and no earring. He left for work every morning in the pickup truck, spoke fondly of squirrel season, built birdhouses and taught me how to shoot a rifle before I was big enough to hold it by myself.

My mom had longer hair, wore earrings when she went to church, smelled nice and worked just as hard as Daddy, but didn't leave home to do it. She was the one waiting for my sister and me at home after school with warm cookies and a hug. She also tried hard to keep me out of trees long enough to teach me to sew, but the sight of a needle and thread reduced me to fits of weeping, which is still the case today.

In the 90's, the gender lines are much harder to define. Men wear ponytails and earrings, cook meals, take time off from work to stay home with the children, buy groceries and empty the kitty litter. Some men admit they have feelings, and some men can even express them. I know a man who actually knows how to sob.

Women crop their hair, wear neckties and suits if they feel like it, leave for work in four-wheel-drive vehicles, go drinking with their buddies after work, and commit violent crimes with alarming regularity.

Since we all have a combination of masculine and feminine characteristics, it's healthy for us to learn to be comfortable with all facets of our personalities. We can evolve to the highest degree when we accept both the masculine and the feminine in ourselves; aside from the obvious anatomically correct features, there sometimes appear to be only a few remaining areas which separate men and women, but they're critical.

Asking for directions is still something only women will do; men will drive aimlessly for hours pretending they're exploring a new route, calculating mileage or thinking deep cosmic thoughts about the nature of man and machine, forged together in the purposeful pursuit of freedom on the open road.

And men clearly don't understand bonding through shopping. I don't know a single man who would call his best friend and say, "Hey, Spike, guess what? I just got this great suit on sale. Come on over and try it on. It'll look great with your new loafers." Men won't have their colors done, they'll never wear pearls, and men won't go to the bathroom together when they're out for dinner. Men never refuse to go out for a beer because their hair looks terrible, and they don't read *Field and Stream* to find out how to identify their T-Zones.

But what finally separates men and women is emotions. Women can express their emotions much more easily than men can. Nobody taught me that it was a gender crime to reveal my feelings or cry. It was accepted as an honest expression of hurt, anger, grief or joy, and I wish boys had been allowed the same freedom. Maybe it would help us all when we grow up and sometimes love each other so badly.

Hit The Road, Jack

Five months ago I wrote him a letter that went something like this:

"Dear Jack,

I like this relationship. It's not unlike the relationship I have with the Queen of England, Clint Eastwood and the Pope—we never see each other and we never talk. The only difference is that neither of the three of them breezed into my life again after five years, turned it upside down and then disappeared again. I know all the reasons, of course. This is a script I've written, edited and rewritten a dozen times. You play your part perfectly because you know I would have nothing to do with Mr. Right unless he were disguised as Mr. Worst Nightmare, and you've won the prize more than once for having created a flawless impersonation of Mr. Right.

So I fell for it again. Not surprising, since it's reasonably well-documented that when it comes to matters of the heart, my learning curve leaves a lot to be desired. Nonetheless, I have a bulletin for you: I have at last realized that you are never prepared to take the consequences of your actions, and, in fact, you never even think about the consequences of your actions. So, I have set myself free of this epic emotional misadventure once and for all."

A few nights ago, he called.

"Hello," he said, as if he had just talked to me yesterday instead of five months ago. "Look, I know I hurt you and I didn't mean to. I wouldn't hurt you for anything in the world. But you're just as intense as I am, and you hurt me too. Everything overwhelmed me, and I had to stop. We live 900 miles apart, and you're here and I'm there and I don't know what to do about it. I didn't know what to say when I got your letter. But I'm here, and I want to see you.

"Oh, I'm fine, thanks," I said. "And how are you? No, you didn't interrupt anything. I was just immersed in the riveting news that clogging is still alive as a craft. Did you know that in the time it takes to stop needless aging, you can remove unsightly facial hair, clean your oven and find a name you can trust in feminine hygiene?"

"Please don't do this to me," he said. "Talk to me. I'll spend the rest of my life making this up to you. Look, I'm writing poetry again, and I'm not throwing it away like I used to. It's because of you that I can do this now. No one else ever told me I had to take responsibility for my creativity. Do you understand? I'm writing again, because of you. DOESN'T THAT MEAN ANYTHING?"

I thought about that for a minute, and then I said "Sometimes I think Gore Vidal was right when he said no other culture but America could produce Ernest Hemingway and not get the joke. I also think silence is the most effective punctuation, and I'm deeply concerned about the conservative majority on the Supreme Court.

My dog and cat are fine, thank you."

"Okay," he said. "Have it your way. I'll just say what I want to say. I'll start all over again. I'm sorry. I'm crazy about you and I want to start over. All over. Brand new. Pretend we just met. I'm a new person. I'll bring references. You'll love me all over again, but this time it will be different. I promise. TALK TO ME."

"Actually," I said, "My cat, Badman Trouble, is having a psychotic episode right now, but that's nothing new. It must be past his bedtime. He's struggling to get into his little kitty pajamas—his favorites with the little red devils and pitchforks printed all over them. I really should go help him—the buttons make him hyperventilate."

"Fine," he said. "I know you're getting some perverse pleasure out of this, and if that makes you happy, then that's just great. But you can't keep it up forever. I'm going to hang up the phone, and I'm going to call a cab. I'll be there in ten minutes, and I'll change your mind about everything. You'll see. Everything will be all right. I'M COMING OVER."

"Well, great, Jack. That's just fine. Hang up the phone and come right over. Do whatever you want, but just be aware that, unlike the present Supreme Court, I believe in *stare decisis*."

"*Stare decisis?*" he said. "Meaning what?"

"Meaning I stand by things decided. The door stays locked."

No Baby Blues For Me

I'm afraid to leave the house because I read in the paper the other day that another 3.8 million babies are about to be born. I'm afraid to answer the phone because that same article will remind my mother that as far as babies go, I never came up with the goods.

"Just one," she'll say. "That's all I ever asked you for. But what did I get? Grand pets. A shredding machine with a happy tail and a psychotic cat who plays air-guitar. It is not outside the realm of possibility that you could have produced at least one relatively normal grandchild—despite the fact that you go out with a man who gave you clown shoes."

My mother is a real laugh riot.

Mother and I have had this conversation many times. I've tried to explain that I don't dislike kids, it's just that I'm scared to death of them. They arrive with a milky-blue gaze that breaks your heart, and then they make you go crazy. One day you're in a feeding frenzy at all the trendy fern bars around town, then suddenly your Volvo displays the self-congratulatory 'Baby on Board' sign—whose only real purpose is to let the rest of us know that you finally did something to make your mother happy.

This new baby will have feet the size of newborn field mice, but you'll spend $56 on a pair of hightops that Larry Byrd could wear on his thumb. And since babies show a great deal of interest in napping, you'll buy him an Aprica carriage which costs about the same as a small foreign car.

If you bring home over $60 a week, you can't send your kid to a regular school with real kids. You must drive him daily to The Twit School for the Extremely Precious, where, instead of just promising to go to ordinary PTA meetings, you have to swear to organize a benefit for all the underprivileged kids who don't have gold signet rings or polo ponies.

But my fear of the baby-unknown actually stems from far more cosmic and intellectual questions: What would I do if he didn't like Pink Floyd? What if she actually preferred milk over Moosehead? What if she wanted a broom? What if this child didn't like clown shoes? What if the kid wanted to join the NRA? WHAT IF THIS WEREN'T A FUNKY KID?

That's the real problem with kids. If you don't like them, you're stuck. You can't take them back, you can't exchange them and you can't drop them off at the kennel when you have to go out of town. You can't put bowls of food and water on the floor for them because whoever sees you do it will for sure call the cops.

You have to housebreak them with stacks of madras diapers, and they can't ride in the car with their heads stuck out the window. Some kids want to live with you even after they're old enough to start school, and some of them tell you stories at night about things under their bed that scare the daylights out of you. And you can't give them good names like Rowdy or Spot; you have to call them Buffy or Amber or Huxley. I understand some kids like to play catch, but I don't think they're good at fetching.

But I do admire a couple of kids I know who live by their wits because they aren't burdened down with baby Rolexes and Lamborghini Big Wheels. When my four-year-old friend Andy makes his mother cry, he says it's good for her to work through her feelings. He also has a real flair for cheap theatrics. If he thinks anyone in the family is ignoring him, he makes a brave and desperate bid for attention by scaling the outside of their two-story house, dressed appropriately in his Spiderman pajamas.

My favorite kid, Matt, now 15, has had a world-view since he was about two, and even though he is the world's youngest collector of implements of destruction, he has a sweet and sensitive side that breaks my heart. When he was 9, he wrote this ad for the Personals column: Younger Man, Very Handsome, Loving—Seeks Rich, Big-Shouldered Broad. Send picture and financial statement to P.O. Box 110.

Be My Valentine

When I was in elementary school I loved Valentine's Day because it was a simple way to tally up my friends; friends could be added and subtracted precisely by the number and type of valentines I received. My favorites were the homemade heart-shaped almost-rhymes:

"Roses are red,
Violets are blue,
Marianne is a tub of lard,
But I don't think you are.
Your friend, Jerry."

Or,

"Roses are red,
Violets are blue,
If I had a dead rat,
I'd give it to you.
Your friend, Billy."

Other valentine messages skipped the set-up and got right to the point, but often failed to provide enough information to close the deal:

"Be mine, Valentine.

Your friend, Guess Who."

I know now that what I loved about Valentine's Day was its innocence and its honesty—kids don't know about subtlety or "sending signals." Kids either like each other or they don't, and Valentine's Day was the day to put your stake in the ground, one way or the other. It was also a day to get even. And that, too, was innocent and honest because the message was clear and clearly meant to wound. The kid I pushed out of the swing in the third grade retaliated with this:

"Roses are red,

Violets are blue,

You're rotten mean and I hate you.

Lulu"

But like everything having to do with affairs of the heart, Valentine's Day got more complicated as I got older. In high school, it was no longer a simple matter to send a boy a valentine for fear its message would be taken literally, or worse, not taken at all. The only safe thing to do was send valentines to girl friends and/or a steady boyfriend. In college, of course, we were far too sophisticated to ever tell anyone we liked them, and too chicken to ever tell anyone that we didn't like them.

Then marriage made Valentine's Day simple yet again. I always knew what to expect from Spike—ebony chocolates reclining seductively in a red satin heart-shaped box, an armful of roses and a sweet, manufactured card: "For My Wife On Valentine's Day." Then I would be taken out to dinner. Spike would try to act cool despite the fact that his underwear was plastered with hearts and cupids, and I would try not to laugh. And he would always say, sweetly, "Roses are red, violets are blue, these shorts are really stupid and so are you."

While Valentine's Day was probably the only thing that didn't contribute to our divorce, this annual salutation to love wasn't enough to save it, either. I missed Spike a lot on the first Valentine's Day after our divorce; at least I was missing him a lot until the mailman presented me with Spike's first in a continuing valentine series bearing this message: "You're No Longer Mine, But I'm Doing Just Fine."

As time passed, I began to think that, as an adult single person, Valentine's Day was just a confusing combination of high school and college—too grown up to send valentines to girlfriends, and still risky to send valentines to less than serious boyfriends.

Despite all gender ambivalence, the card companies finally caught on and got a grip. Valentines can now be found to express just about any sentiment for any relationship.

Just this week I got a valentine with a timely message from Rocky, my stock-broker friend:
"Roses are red
Violets are blue
We're in a recession,
Yes, dear, it's true.
I've lost all my money,
My laptop's in hock,
My new Saab was stolen,
Along with my piece of the rock.
Nonetheless, I'll be just fine
As long as you are my Valentine."

Spike's valentine came the same day, with his own version of a contemporary message: "For My First Ex-Wife On Valentine's Day."

A Man's Home –
Castle Of Nightmares

When my friends argue about who's the biggest risk-taker among them, I simply smile and wait for their attention to shift to me. "Buried in an avalanche? HA. Chicky and bunny stuff. So you were in a Moroccan jail for two weeks? Big deal. Moroccans do it everyday. And so what if you were making love when the car crashed? Really, that's just bush league."

Oh sure, I've fallen into a river full of piranha in South America, and I've looked into the jaws of a moray eel 85 feet down in the Cayman Islands. I once saw a man shot with a sawed-off shotgun, and I defended myself with a knife once. I've walked in my sleep on the roof of my house, and I've even lied to my mother. I'm also reasonably sure that my cat, Badman Trouble, has a prison record a mile long.

So what if I don't live my life in a cocoon? And I don't care if you've flown over the Grand Canyon wearing nothing but a propeller hat, none of it compares to the risk involved in seeing a man's house for the first time.

I'm not sure how they do it, but some men present

themselves as well-rounded, well-read, intelligent human beings who lead multi-faceted lives filled with interesting people, colorful travel, and rewarding work. Not to mention a well-developed social conscience, a thoughtful world-view and a reasonable tolerance for women who like rare pork roast.

But when I step into their living rooms, two thoughts frequently occur: Either I've stepped onto the dark side of the moon, or sometimes bad things happen to nice men who live alone.

When it comes to how a man lives, I don't ask for much. I don't care about decorator furniture or highly polished surfaces or matching towels. I can barely wade through the clutter in my own house, and the only thing I know about a kitchen is that it's a good place to keep food if you have any, and if you have any, it's a good place to eat it because you can stand over the sink.

All I ask for in a man's house is some books, some music and some evidence of his interests, his work, or his hobbies. Not only is it comforting to know that he can read, but I like some proof that he does. I like to see a fishing hat, or a baseball glove. Or a piano, a camera, a Scrabble game, or a pool cue—anything to add dimension to the sagging armchair in front of the TV doing a great impression of his body.

I might still be friends with a university professor I used to see if he hadn't insisted that I come to his house for dinner. He was highly regarded in the academic community, not only for his near-legendary teaching skills, but for his prolific stream of scholarly essays which always expanded the boundaries of his field.

Despite my dread, I tried to cheer myself with the

thought that an intellectual professor would surround himself with the classics; and I would be sure to hear *La Traviatta* wafting through the windows as I approached his door. I had even convinced myself that his living room would be a showcase for a vast collection of rare musical instruments.

Dream on, fool.

Every piece of furniture in the professor's living room was upholstered in crushed gold velvet, and every surface in the living room was covered with shellacked driftwood and little hollow walnut shells tricked out to look like baby owls. His bedroom, which I viewed from a safe distance in the hallway, was painted black. I'm sure he chose black because he thought it was a tasteful contrast to the throbbing disco glitter ball hanging from the ceiling. Something called 'musical massage' throbbed along on the stereo.

There were no books in sight, unless you count the stacks of the well-worn journals of popular culture with their centerfolds stapled in the stomach, or the 2,000 page *COMPLETE INTERGALACTIC GUIDE TO CABLE TV— EVERY LISTING FOR EVERY STATION IN THE UNIVERSE EVERY MINUTE OF EVERY DAY.*

When dinner was announced, I said I was really sorry, but I couldn't possibly stay because I'd been suddenly struck by a recurrent terminal illness. In fact, I was so sick I had to go to the bathroom and throw up before I could leave.

He seemed genuinely disappointed, but he said he was glad I'd at least get to see his most prized possessions before I left.

"How bad could it be?" I thought as I staggered toward

the bathroom. Maybe there's a tiny disco dance floor in there, or maybe the bathroom scale is rigged up to a neon sign flashing the message, "There's Just More of You To Love," or maybe the commode plays the *William Tell Overture* when the top is lifted.

Any of those would have been an improvement over what I found. Every wall in the bathroom was covered, floor to ceiling, with his prized collection of airline barf bags—one from every airline in the world, it seemed.

Getting sick never felt so good.

D-I-V-O-R-C-E
Film At 11

Most of us know that marriage is the leading cause of divorce, but who can explain the growing trend toward public divorces? It seems that the more prominent the individuals involved, the more private the wedding and the more public the divorce.

Lack of money explains why Spike and I had a small wedding, but we also had a small divorce—attended only by a shared lawyer, who, when it was all said and done, divided up the proceeds equally. It's been a long time, but I recall his having said something lofty and lawyer-like as he presented us with the financial rewards of our broken dreams: "It comes down to about $14.32 each; don't spend it all in one place."

That was, of course, after his fees and court costs.

We each did what we thought best at the time. Spike gave me a divorce present—a gold band—from which three thin gold rings, each set with a tiny diamond, circled each other freely—floating around a tiny post. It's been a long time, but I recall his having said something profoundly poetic as he presented me with this token of our broken dreams: "It reminded me of you. It's unusual, it's one of a kind, and it goes around in circles."

Sentimental fool that I am, I thanked him through my tears, fervently kissed him good-bye, and asked him to please fall off the face of the earth forever.

But, as divorces go, ours was as good as they get. Making the decision to get a divorce was painful and agonizing for both of us, but once we agreed, the divorce itself was swift, simple and private.

Granted, two things were in our favor in terms of simplicity—we had no children and nothing of real value to dispose of other than our house—which, on any given month, could have been the featured selection in *Architectural Unrest*. But even if the divorce hadn't been simple, I still think we would have kept it private.

But these days it seems fewer people are invited to witness the joy and promise of the wedding, but when it's time for divorce, it's film at 11.

Celebrities, of course, are notorious for their secret weddings and public divorces. But who can really blame them for having such explosive divorces? Their weddings are kept so secret that they probably have no idea who they're supposed to marry in the first place. No wonder Sean Penn is always so angry—maybe he thought he was going to marry the girl who sat in front of him in algebra.

But it's the truly exclusive society weddings and truly messy society divorces that really take the prize:

"Mr. and Mrs. Olivier Merriweather Purringfurr IV announce the forthcoming marriage of their daughter, Miss Felicity Anne "Whiskers" Purringfurr, to Mr. Rock On June 21, 1992, at 6 p.m. at the Adath United Holy Roller Cathedral Synagogue in Newport, R.I. The bride and groom will be attended by President and Mrs. George Bush.

"Miss Purringfurr and Mr. On have purchased Boston, Mass., where they plan to make their home. Miss Purringfurr will continue in her capacity as Chief Executive Officer of Intergalactic Media Conglomerates, Inc., and Mr. On will continue to study for his GED, after which he will devote his time to the poor."

About 18 months will pass, then the supermarket tabloids trumpet the news: "WHISKERS AND ROCK CALL IT QUITS." The accompanying story will contain a tasteful statement issued by Whiskers' press secretary: "I have inter-office memo paper with a higher IQ than his. He signed a prenuptial agreement, and even though he couldn't read it, he agreed to keep his mitts off my money." This is followed by a tasteful statement from Rock's press secretary: "That bum. Who does she think she is? I want all her money so's I can give it to the poor," signed "Miffed in Boston."

Six months later, the tabloids report the conclusion: "PURRINGFURR FORTUNE WIPED OUT BY LEGAL FEES; ROCK GETS CHECK FOR $14.32"

It's been a long time, but I can still remember the prenuptial agreement that Spike and I had—"No matter what happens between us, we'll just work it out, OK?"

Doctor, Doctor

My friend Martini and I were having dinner the other night when she suddenly started to sniffle. At first I thought the chef had put too much thyme in the soufflé, but then her eyes got red and she started to shake.

"Martini, what's wrong?" I asked, alarmed. It suddenly struck me that she might have the Shanghai flu, a particularly vitriolic strain that reached epidemic proportions around the country during March and April.

"Martini, do you have the Shanghai flu, a particularly vitriolic…"

"Stop it," Martini coughed. "I do not have the flu. I'm perfectly fine. It must be spring fever. After all, it is May and the buds are bursting out all over."

"Martini, spring fever affects the heart. It does not give you a hacking cough, fever, chills and, judging by the pale-green tint in your cheeks, impending nausea."

"Oh, look!" she said. "There's George and Barbara Bush over there. Let's go and say hello. I didn't know they were in town, did you? Maybe they're here early for the Derby. You know how George loses track of things. He probably thinks it's..."

"Martini, stop babbling," I said. "You're sick and I've figured out what's wrong with you, so you may as well stop avoiding the issue."

Martini lifted her chin and gave me a baleful glare while she idly carved hearts in my meatloaf.

"Martini," I said, "Let's face it. You've got a near-terminal case of the Love Flu."

Martini recoiled as if she'd been struck, but I plunged ahead. "Look, you're in a non-productive relationship characterized by an obsessive desire to be with the wrong person and you're suffering alternating fits of feverish exhilaration followed by chilling depression. Your obsessive-compulsive behavior is generating feelings of low self-esteem and complete unworthiness."

"Oh, would you excuse me a minute?" Martini said. "There's Bill and Hillary. I really do want to go say hello. I haven't seen them for ages."

"Martini, sit down. You shouldn't be ashamed of this. The Love Flu has hit just about everyone I know this year. Maybe it's because we're on the cusp of a new decade, or maybe it's because we're moving into the Age of Aquarius, or, who knows, maybe it's just Fear of the Subjunctive. But when Jo Ella had the Love Flu, she called the Center for Disease Control, and they told her what to do."

Martini was busy waving at Al and Tipper, so I pinned her hand to the table with my fork.

"Listen, Mart, these people are professionals. They told Jo Ella that Love Flu is rarely fatal unless it's a Gemini/Virgo combination. You can have a complete recovery if you accept the fact that a relationship that

stimulates interest without promoting deeper understanding is not going to last."

Suddenly Martini focused her full attention on me.
"Look who's talking," she said. "If anyone could
recognize the symptoms of Love Flu, it would certainly be
you—the intergalactic expert on non-productive
relationships. Last summer you fell face forward into the
abyss with your usual disregard as to where it would lead,
and then a few months later you suffered a depth-charge
to the heart because you blinded yourself to the fact that
this man does not understand that a relationship requires
some assembly.

"And stop ignoring me," Martini said, gathering herself
up for the kill. "It's time to heal yourself. You may not
have known better the first time, but you fell for it again,
even after he told you he couldn't be trusted. So were your
best friends surprised when you got hurt all over again?
Boy, I may have the Love Flu, but you need a brain trans-
plant. The only thing you can't do in excess is
moderation."

I took a deep breath and looked Martini in the eye.
"Would you excuse me for a minute?" I said. "I just saw
Nelson and Winnie Mandela come in, and I haven't seen
him since he got out of jail. I really should go say hello."

Let's Get Personal

My friend Lassie asked me recently what I would do if I decided I wanted a mate. "A mate?" I said. "Why do you ask? Is it mating season? Did I miss the only fun event ever offered for singles? Actually, I thought only gloves have mates. And shoes. We know that socks, being completely without moral fiber, mate indiscriminately, but people..."

Her eyes started to glaze over, so I shifted the burden and asked what she would do if she wanted a mate. She declared without hesitation that she would write a personals ad. So would I, I mused, if my name were Lassie.

Generally, we think of advertising as a way to sell simple things like beer and cars and hamburgers and political candidates. The notion of advertising yourself through a personals ad is a daunting concept: Take the most complicated product ever invented, the human being, and reduce its essence to a few key selling points in three lines of type and run it in a special section in the back of a newspaper or magazine.

Wait a few days, and then you can sit cross-legged on

your bed and review the hopefuls without going into the singles' danger zones—bars and supermarkets. And not only that; you can imperiously toss the inferior ones in the wastebasket. Or if you're a real hard case, you can stamp 'REJECT' on their pictures and paper the basement with them.

Is this a great country or what?

Personal ads have been picking up steam since Miles Standish met Pricilla Mullens in *The Plymouth Rock Gazette:* "Howdy, Pilgrim. Stranger in town seeks Puritan lady of gentle breeding. Send note, photo to John Alden." But there are some things you should know before you put yourself up for sale or before you respond to "Gorgeous, leggy blonde seeks male companionship. No one walks away."

First, creative writing works for the advertiser because you can turn your undesirable characteristics into selling points. But if you're the respondent, the only way to avoid disappointment is to be adept at interpreting the creative writing. For instance, "Well-secured man with steady job, gentled and devoid of sharp edges, seeks lovely woman who likes occasional trips to the country" translates to axe-murderer in prison wants a nice lady for weekly visitation.

Or, "Strong, independent woman looking for sensitive, warm, caring, thoughtful man. Must be willing to compromise." This is a power-hungry witch looking for a punching bag who can double as a doorstop.

This ad, "Daring, adventurous athlete who loves cycling looking for warm woman to hold onto," was placed by an Iron Horseman looking for an old lady.

Beware of ads placed by men who say they're looking for a woman who "must love children." That's his way of telling you that he's already supporting at least five.

This one, "Brilliant, stunning, accomplished ocean-ographer/author/composer/brain surgeon seeks mate of equal standing," simply means it takes one to know one.

It's also important to be able to recognize the truly desperate: "Man seeks woman. All responses given due consideration." Or, "Terrific Renaissance lady looking for companionship and ambient body temperature. Can operate all modern life-support systems."

In addition to creative writing and interpretation, the other thing to consider in writing your ad is targeted marketing. This means writing your ad in such a way that you attract responses from a very specific group; or you can write the same ad in different ways to appeal to different audiences.

To illustrate, here are two ads I wrote for myself:

"Intelligent pre-married professional enjoys billiards and percussive music. Favorite aerobic sports are speed-reading and big-dog walking; fond of high-speed leading-edge transportation and animated artwork. Would enjoy male companionship focused on similar interests."

Rewritten, a new target market is revealed:

"Divorced dog-lover, likes to shoot pool, play drums and drive fast. Can also read good and has job. Would like to watch cartoons with man who has his own pool cue and rock band."

All responses given due consideration.

The Last Wedding

For years now, the mere thought of getting married again was enough to make me weep. In fact, even while I was married, the realization that I was married often made me weep. I associated marriage with pain and compromise and a constant struggle to be myself, to guard my freedom, my individuality and my right to be one as opposed to half of a couple.

I set aside all thought of marriage because I carried a vow deep in my heart that I would never compromise again—never settle for less than exactly what I wanted, or felt I deserved, from somcone who might be my husband. And since I'd set the hurdle so high, I just assumed it would never happen again.

But it did.

I married Michael Stamper on May 13 at the Hall of Justice. The wedding ceremony was much like our courtship—swift, heartfelt, slightly surreal and absolutely hilarious.

We decided to get married at the Hall Of Justice when we found out that getting married in Kentucky is much like going through a drive-in restaurant. You stop at the courthouse to place your order, then you run over to the Hall of Justice to pick it up. No waiting period, no blood tests. All you have to do is show up at the courthouse with a picture I.D., the date of your divorce, $22.50 for the license (only $15 for a Hunting and Fishing license if you change your mind), and the ability to answer a few questions that could have been written by the Marx Brothers.

Right after the "what is your occupation?" question, and the "when did you get divorced?" question, there followed the and-now-for-something-completely-different question: "Are you related to each other?"

My first thought was, WHAT? Do we look slightly blue? Do we look like double first cousins? Are we celebrating Chromosome Conservation Week?

Upon reflection, I realized this is a perfectly reasonable question to ask of people getting married in Kentucky.

After having provided the correct response to that question (if we'd said yes, would we have been awarded the Governor's Medal for Genetic Conservation?), we took our license and set off across the street to the Hall of Justice.

We arrived at the designated marrying place, along with two friends, to find two other couples waiting for any available judge to perform the ceremony. But there were no judges available—they were all otherwise engaged fighting crime and/or evil.

And so we waited. Thirty or forty minutes passed while Michael and I mostly looked at each other—happy and awe-struck that barely three months of courtship had propelled us to this moment. The other two couples approached wedlock a bit differently: One man slept through the entire waiting period while his wife-to-be stared into the distance, silently telegraphing a message I interpreted as RABBIT DIED, RABBIT DIED. The other man telegraphed a sentiment which could not be misinterpreted—he wore a T-shirt imprinted with this message: Simon says Go - - - - Yourself.

Finally we were all ushered into an empty courtroom and told that a judge would be with us shortly. One of the judges rushed in a few minutes later, looking slightly harried but making a fine judicial fashion statement in his long black robe. He apologized for the delay, and for the fact that, since he'd had to leave his court in mid-session, he only had time to marry all of us at the same time.

We were all a lovely couple.

We all lined up and I stood between Michael and the man who summed up his world-view on his T-shirt. The judge, despite his breathless state, gave his prenuptial instruction with feeling and humor. (It's just as legal to get married all at once, he said; just don't look at the wrong person when you say "I do").

So the six of dutifully repeated our vows in unison, and we were all doing so well that at some point I wasn't sure if we were getting married or becoming U. S. citizens. Shortly thereafter the judge pronounced us all married, although we weren't sure to whom, but at least I know I left with the man I want to spend the rest of my life with.